Tom Hood, William Jeffery Prowse

Nicholas's Notes and Sporting Prophecies

with some miscellaneous poems, serious and humorous

Tom Hood, William Jeffery Prowse

Nicholas's Notes and Sporting Prophecies
with some miscellaneous poems, serious and humarous

ISBN/EAN: 9783337402495

Printed in Europe, USA, Canada, Australia, Japan

Cover: Foto ©Andreas Hilbeck / pixelio.de

More available books at **www.hansebooks.com**

NICHOLAS'S NOTES,

AND

SPORTING PROPHECIES,

WITH SOME

MISCELLANEOUS POEMS, SERIOUS AND HUMOROUS.

BY THE LATE W. J. PROWSE.

EDITED, WITH A BRIEF BIOGRAPHICAL NOTICE,
BY TOM HOOD.

LONDON:
GEORGE ROUTLEDGE AND SONS,
THE BROADWAY, LUDGATE.

BENTLEY AND CO., PRINTERS, SHOE LANE, LONDON.

A MEMOIR OF THE LATE W. J. PROWSE.

THE records of the life of a literary man, like WILLIAM JEFFERY PROWSE, are almost invariably uneventful. The victories of the pen are won in the silence and seclusion of the study; although their effect is at least as wide-spread and as important as that of the more conspicuous achievements of the sword. Moreover, in the ranks of the Press Militant, the captain is as little known to the public as the private soldier;—the most brilliant leader-writer, except amongst his immediate friends and fellow-workers, is as unrecognized as the reporter of fires, suicides, and police cases. Of the thousands of readers, whom his clear reason had influenced, who had been fascinated by the charm of his style, scarcely one understood all that was meant by the simple announcement of the death of William Jeffery Prowse. Nevertheless, I will not allow these few of his literary remains to be published without a brief chronicle of his life.

He was born on the 6th of May, 1836, at Torquay, in Devonshire; his love for which beautiful county is evidenced in a poem of his, "Devonshire Worthies,"

4 MEMOIR.

contributed in 1855 to *The Western Times*. After the death of his father, about 1844, he was adopted by his uncle, Mr. John Sparke Prowse, a notary-public and ship-broker, residing at Greenwich. It was intended that he should become a notary, but he abandoned the idea when he was claimed by the Press, which, as Mr. Hannay admirably remarked in his memoir of Father Prout, irresistibly draws to it its chosen recruits, no matter what their original occupation may be.

He first went to a school kept by Mr. Wanostrocht —the "Felix" of cricket chronicles; but was subsequently transferred to another school in Greenwich. He began to write early—in 1851, I believe—for he inherited literary tastes from his mother, who was an intimate friend of Keats, and who contributed to the annuals, and published a volume of poems, as Miss Marianne Jeffery. *Chambers's Journal*, the *Ladies' Companion*, and the *National Magazine*, were the periodicals in which his first literary work was done. He served his apprenticeship to journalism in the columns of the *Aylesbury News*.* In 1861, he was engaged upon the *Daily Telegraph*, his first article in which would appear to be a report of the Oxford and Cambridge boat-race, while his last important contribution was a leader on the death of Tom Lockyer, the cricketer.

Although his health was always delicate, he was

* I find among his papers a rough copy of verses for it about "King Clicquot," dated 1855, which wind up with this couplet :—

"His courtiers found him out at last beneath the table sunk,
Problematically pious, but indubitably drunk."

It is not every lad of twenty who can pen as neat and smart a line as that last.

devoted to manly sports, and took an especial delight in cricket. In the last two years of his life, when a confirmed invalid, he found his greatest enjoyment in watching the matches at The Oval. For him, as for Pope also, the mystery and danger of Arctic exploration had a strange fascination. His library contained almost all the books of Polar Travels, and he often expressed a wish that he could join an expedition to the North. I can remember a friend's telling him that he believed the height of his ambition was to play a game of cricket on an ice-field, with the Pole for a wicket! He had an intense love for the sea, on which a great-uncle had seen service, who was Flag-Lieutenant of the "Ajax," at the Battle of Trafalgar. When he left England for Nice, last autumn, though much debilitated, he preferred to make the journey on a sailing-vessel to Marseilles, to the amazement of those of his friends, who could not understand that love of the sea which made him appreciate so thoroughly the lines in Thomas Hood's sonnet, "To Ocean" :—

> " My absent friends talk in thy very roar,
>   In thy waves' beat their kindly pulse I see,
> And, if I must not see my England more,
>   Next to her soil my grave be found in thee ! "*

Alas, the grave of William Jeffery Prowse is in the cemetery at Nice !

To the outside world, which is satisfied with the knowledge that its newspaper will be on its breakfast-

---

* Of his copy of Hood's Works, he writes that, " In sickness— and with sickness my acquaintance is particularly close—they are a never-failing source of amusement,—and of consolation, too, by the by ; the wisdom lies so close to the wit, and both, by some derange- ment of ordinary anatomies, come so directly from the heart."

table as punctually as the milk and the rolls, the fact
that a man is on the sub-editorial staff of a daily journal means very little. Nobody seems to reflect that it
implies night-long labour, anxious and wearisome, in an
unhealthy atmosphere. It was this work that told upon
poor Prowse's constitution, and developed symptoms
which, in 1865, compelled him to seek medical advice.
Writing to a friend in the spring of that year, he says:
"I had a long talk with Dr. Jenner. That cough of mine,
with which I must have often bored you, has connections,
look you, and relations with one of my 'Principal Contents,' viz., that lung which is in the left part of my
chest. Don't say much about this business of mine,
for I have a strong objection to lying down on my back
and howling for sympathy." Dr. Jenner ordered him
to South Devon, where he stayed with an uncle at his
native place, Torquay. The rest and the change did him
great good. In March he writes:—"Your dream of
literature and liberty and love all 'in a cottage' should
not, delightful as it is, be too much to realize. Thank
Heaven we have got out of the Grub Street days—which
ought, I fancy, to be called the *no*-Grub Street days!—
and every man of brains who is also a man of honour
can do well enough so long as he is careful of his stock-
in-trade; that stock-in-trade, so charmingly portable,
over which he places his hat and draws his right-hand
glove every morning. Hurrah, then, for ——, where,
left-lung permitting, I hope to blow my 'bacco, and to
make ill-natured remarks about sham-great men, and utter
incoherent enthusiasms about Gladstone, Abd-el-Kader,
Schamyl, Garibaldi, and Robert Lee. *And the left lung
will, I think, permit!*" With this leisure and with
returning health, his active mind was busily planning

work for the future :—" I have plotted here a couple of books, but my novel, although I have lots of the characters and some situations, hasn't crystallized yet into order; and I don't want to force it. I meditate—1st, ' The Boats : a Book for Boys.' Jolly subject, if not yet done. Raleigh up the Orinoco, Bligh, Franklin's earlier trips, the life-boats, Nelson's cutting-outs, Cochrane, etc., etc. 2nd, ' Bohemia in England and France ' —literary criticism and biography; a good deal of it already written, and only needing a little revision. I have a good deal of rather out-of-the-way reading on the subject." ..... " The sensation of having nothing to do is rather bewildering at first. I am not absolutely used to entire inactivity, but I think I shall manage to keep myself from becoming disgusted with a little rest."

Unfortunately, the improvement in health was but temporary. He returned to London and to labour, but in the succeeding—indeed, in every subsequent—winter the malady increased, until, in the autumn of 1867, he consulted Dr. Williams, who at once ordered him to winter at Nice. He had to stay some weeks at Broadstairs to gather strength for the journey, and left early in November. He spent the winter at Cimiès, near Nice, and returned in the spring, better, apparently, although much enfeebled. Fortunately, at this time he was residing with his aunt, who died last November, and whose friend and companion, Miss Ashenden, having known him since the time when they were brought up together as children, nursed him with the tender solicitude and unwearying affection of a sister. The next winter found him again at Cimiès, whither he returned once more in the autumn of '69. His weakness had increased, and the gravest fears were entertained for

him.   But though it seems probable that he felt the end
was near, he maintained a cheerful exterior, and inspired
his friends with hopes never to be realized.   During his
residence abroad he kept a brief diary—mere notes of
that important matter to him, the weather, with memo-
randums of his work in frequent entries of "Wrote."
On the 20th of December comes the ominous entry,
"Rode for two hours, but gravely ill afterwards.   Took
cold."   On the 23rd I read, "Cold.   Telegram, Tom
Lockyer's death."   And from that time, day after day,
"cold" or "bitterly cold" occurs, to show how much
the season was against him.   On the 31st he wrote, with
a feeling of sadness he would have concealed from his
friends in speaking, "Here, thank God, ends a miserable
year!"   On the 16th of January the diary closes :—"the
rest is silence!"

    "When he was taken ill in January," writes a kindly
Englishman who was with him to the last, "and there
was some fear that he might go off after a fit of cough-
ing, he wrote some farewell messages"—a few words in
pencil to three or four of his most intimate friends.—
"His end was very peaceful. . . . . This winter I have seen
a good deal of him, and have been astonished at the
wonderful cheerfulness and patience with which he has
borne his sufferings"—of which, to the very last, he
strove to spare those at home the knowledge.   His death
took place on Easter Sunday.

    As a writer he was gifted with a great charm of
style.   With a fertile imagination, he possessed a severely
logical mind.   The amount of work he has done is
astonishing.   Knowing, as I did, how incessantly he
worked, writing often two, and at times three, leaders a
day, I was surprised to find volume after volume filled

with his articles, carefully cut out and pasted-in. And yet, amidst this constant and fatiguing toil, he found time to write poems, and essays, and papers for the magazines, the annuals, and *Fun*.

I must not omit mention of his wonderful faculty of imitation, as displayed in his "Prize Essays," and a series of papers published in the *Porcupine*, in which he imitated the principal writers of the day—not by parodying particular passages, but by assimilating their habits of thinking and writing. The famous "Rejected Addresses" are not more cleverly and perfectly done. His letters were charming, full of humour and kindliness. In conversation, which he was too modest to try to monopolize, he was a delightful talker. I can remember how, at a friend's house, where there used to be a weekly gathering of workers in literature and art, he would throw in quietly a few words, and then hang down his head as if he were ashamed of them; but at the end of the evening, when one recalled the talk, one found that the best and brightest thing had been said by "Jeff Prowse," as we who loved him called him!

Of his private character and disposition, some idea may be gathered from a passage in a letter I received but recently from a friend :—" Poor Prowse! The best fellows I ever knew have had somebody who hated and privately abused them—except Prowse." He must, indeed, have been loveable of whom that can be said, in a world where one's best intentions are misinterpreted, one's best actions maligned. Every man who associated with him will remember while he lives—

> "The friend he knew
> So gentle and so generous, and so true!"

Gentle, generous, and true—unselfish, brave, loyal,

and loveable, he will not be soon or easily forgotten. And if it is sad to think that a friend is gone, it is no less sad to reflect that the world has lost a great writer. If this young man—barely thirty-four—has left behind him such marks of genius, what might not literature have gained from him at a riper age! And yet such a life as his has not been lived in vain. Short as was his stay among us, thousands of readers have felt the power of that keen intellect, have been influenced by the teaching of that clear brain: while of those who knew and loved him, there is not one, I am sure, who will not acknowledge himself the better for the example of that gentle, brave, honest life.

T. H.

INTRODUCTORY.

It is by no means apologetically that I remind the reader how the NICHOLAS PAPERS were written week by week, in the brief intervals of arduous and engrossing journalistic work. On the contrary, I mention the fact, because it should increase one's admiration for the genius, which, under such circumstances, and from materials so slight, could create the life-like character of "The Old Man." For it is not merely to his quaint language and ingenious blundering that NICHOLAS owes his popularity; but to those masterly little touches, by which he is made to reveal himself, autobiographically, in all his cunning and all his meanness,—servile in adversity, ungrateful in prosperity, vain, mendacious, and disreputable. Yet with all this, he has some indescribable quality which compels us in spite of ourselves to own to a sneaking kindness for "the old thief." Surely, a creation like this might have been not unworthy even of the pen which drew Captain Costigan.

The Miscellanies appended to the NICHOLAS PAPERS will serve to display their writer's powers in a far dif-

ferent field. Their tenderness, their kindly humour,
their touching pathos, will sufficiently commend them ;
but I would ask the reader to reflect what we might
have expected from the mature genius of one who,
dying at the early age of thirty-four, has yet left such
poems behind him.

I must not conclude this preface without expressing
my thanks to Mr. T. Scott for his kindness in drawing,
and to the Messrs. Dalziel, who were good enough to
engrave, the admirable portrait which forms the frontis-
piece.

T. H.

NICHOLAS'S NOTES.

Exclusive Engagement of Nicholas.

With feelings of considerable pride we inform our readers that we have been enabled (at some expense) to secure the exclusive services of the celebrated Nicholas. Nicholas was originally (we are sure he won't object to our saying so) emphatically a son of the people, with no father in particular to look after him; but, like the memorable Murray and the gifted Longman, he made his fortune by his books; and, like George Stephenson, his wealth is identified with the progress of metallics. Raised by his general abilities and his particular obstinacy about Blair Athol to a pitch of prosperity which is faintly represented by the term Belgravia, Nicholas, that friend of man, has benevolently consented to impart (for a certain weekly stipend) the experience of—well, let us say, *middle* age to the generous ardour of youth; AND THIS IS HOW HE DOES IT:

Belgravia.

Sir,—To your own Nicholas lucre have long been comparatively indifferent, and if I now accept your

offer, it is less with a view to personal emolument than
to the generally creditable nature of the concern. My
snug but capacious abode have long been environed by
the emissaries of the great.   Rich I am ; richer I might
have been, if polluted and venal; but, sir, he will
honestly do his best to land your noble sportsmen on
the right shore of the River Stakes like a Sharon,
which, if classical allusions seem inaccurate, drop one
and carry two. His (N.'s) pen is somewhat out of
practice, or would now dash off a few lines of poetical
prophecy ; but I have been myself informed as impromp-
twos is seldom done under two days' notice.

At the general election I start for Parliament.

But still, bless you, I haven't a bit of pride about
me, and the tip at present is—Breadalbane, Gladiateur,
Oppressor.

Mind, this tip may be altered; personally my bets
will be different.

NICHOLAS.

THE DERBY.

BELGRAVIA.

Descriptive writing being less my province than
knowing a really good horse when I see him, and have
been thrown off by a-many in my time, though, thanks
be, still hale and hearty for his age, NICHOLAS will not
attempt to paint our national sports and customs which,
even had he the pen of a *Kelly's Post Office Directory*,
would be too numerous for insertion.

After the numerous Derbys which your sporting
editor have attended, usually in a humble way, though

never menial, whatever envious prophets may insinuate, and when I was younger, before misfortunes, could have his glass of sherry wine where others were only too glad to get their half-pint of four-ale, it is with some amount of pardonable pride that I shall go down in my "own drag," with some of the noblest in the land a-bowing to me, as affable as oil, when they see the old man, which well they know his word was ever as good as his bond, and frequently better, whenever times was bad. It's money as makes the mare to go— mares reminding me of Friday and the Oaks, which will bring me back to original subject, so excuse digression.

Well, my noble sportsmen, trust your own old tipster when he tells you where to put the pot on, and will now cast his eyes down the whole boiling of the horses on the card.

Should Gladiateur keep his Two Thousand form, the stakes may go to our lively neighbours, *les Francais;* and NICHOLAS hopes he have rose above the meanness of being jealous when a foreign *gentilhomme*—or, as he might say, *noble homme*, though his French is not what it was—wins a great prize upon the turf of *vieux Angleterre.*

Space preventing further criticism, will abstain from absolute prophecy, but will give the novice a little hint :—If you back *all* the horses that run, you are sure to win something or other. The plan, of course, requires capital, and you mightn't get paid after all ; but

THERE IS NO OTHER GOLDEN RULE FOR SUCCESS UPON THE TURF.

NICHOLAS.

GLADIATEUR ! GLADIATEUR ! ! GLADIATEUR ! ! !

BELGRAVIA.

Well, my noble sportsmen, and how do we find ourselves to-day? Tolerably brisk, I fancy, sanguineous
and placid! The astounding success with which it have
pleased the will of Fate to reward for the hundredth
occasion the sagacity and intelligence of your own
prophet is by this time—to quote the gifted bard of
Avon—familiar in men's mouths as all the year round;
and my reputation, always a good one, whatever detrac-
tors may now say, to whom in former years many is
the glass of warm gin and water I have generously
stood, is now brighter than ever. Self-praise butters
no parsnips; and it is far from the wish of NICHOLAS to
be vanity-glorious or boastful. Still, modesty is one
thing, and will back himself to possess as much of that
virtue as any man of my age and weight, Irish only
excepted; but it is quite another guess sort of matter
to deliberately go putting your light underneath of a
bushel of hay, whether insured or otherwise. Why was
talents given us if not that we might use them for the
benefit of our fellow-men and squaring up our own
books? Answer that!

My Derby victory of this year is certainly amongst
my most brilliant triumphs.

Likely as not, there may be found some detractorial
whipper-snappers, whom I wouldn't touch with my
hunting-gloves on, nor demean myself by calling of
them all the most awful names as I can lay my tongue
to, who will point out to you, Mr. Editor, in anonymous
letters, that in Number Three of the New Serious I didn't
absolutely name Gladiateur to win.

Look back, sir, to your own file in the back office, and turn to Number Two of the New Serious. Do you find the name of Gladiateur *there*, or is the old man a-trying to conoodle you, as he may say ?

You *do* find the name of Gladiateur given as a winner; and if your printer, as is a deal too fond of altering my contributions on account of alleged errors in stile and authorgraphy, hadn't taken it upon himself to reverse the order in which I sent my tip, and put a " 2 " to Gladiateur's name instead of a " 1," which such it was in the original manuscript, why even the voice of slander would now be hushed on land and sea, and the poisoned fangs of a carroty calumniator, since I can give no higher term to young Dick Jones, as called me a muff in the paddock itself, would long since have subsided into their native element—contempt ! And if he didn't know I was getting old, like a foul-mouthed social nuisance which he is, and his father kep a beer-shop in the New Cut, would have thought twice before he hurled the arrows of Invective against the honour-able head of Age !

But no one—not even yourself, Mr. Editor, nor any of your staff, than whom, I am sure, a more amiable and affable body of young gentlemen, although perhaps a little extravagant and gay, but youth will be served— can make a silk purse out of a sow's ear, and a sow's ear is only too eulogious a patteringmimic for such as Jones.

Want of space—the room given to sportive matter in your otherwise well-conducted journal not being adequate to the importance of the subject—forbids your prophet from giving you this present week

ANY PROPHECY AT ALL.

NICHOLAS.

P.S.—I had almost forgotten to say that although as a tipster I exult, as a patriotic British statesman I deplore. O England, O my country!

THE GRAND PRIX DE PARIS.—ASCOT ANTICIPATIONS.

PARIS, THE GRAND HOTEL, *Monday, June* 12.

Vive la France! Ever since I left my native shore, with the exception of a brief but tumultuous interval of stomachic misery on board the packet, your Prophet has had a remarkably good time of it, never having been in Paris before, circumstances pecuniary and social being rather against him until recent luck.

Paris—the Looteacher Parisionum of the ancients—has been so often described, that NICHOLAS will not detain your readers by details concerning of manners and customs, since such must be expected as different in foreign parts, and which instead of their flim-flam and their kickshaws, give *me* a honest joint and a good glass of sherry wine!

With a paganism which NICHOLAS will not attempt to extenuate nor set down in malice, the Grand Race was held yesterday (Sunday), but am bound to say, in spite of such profanity, and which I am told is habitual, the people were most well-conducted and more sober than is usual on a race-course amongst a contiguous people much given to speak of the French as "our lively neighbours."

You will already have heard the result of the race from other and earlier sources of information, and which what I allude to is the electric fluid. The victory again fell to my old favourite—to that horse which I have stood through thick and thin, regardless of calumny, and too proud to hedge, namely, videlicet,

GLADIATEUR.

I think I predicted as much in my contribution to Number Five of the New Serious, but not having a file of the paper by me in this foreign clime, cannot say positive. I know I meant to, at any rate, and, personally, I backed him heavy.

After the race, I went to an International banquet and plenty of champagne, but the old man was cautious, Mr. Editor, and stuck to his sherry wine.

It was at this dinner that I gave my Ascot tip. Of course time alone can show whether it will prove successful; but you are tolerably well aware by this time, I should fancy, that the old man is not a fool.

"Messieurs," I said, "unaccoutomé comme je suis au publique parlant, c'est avec grande émotion que je rise. Quant au Coupe de l'Ascot, le Général Peel est un bon cheval; mais Ely est un meilleur. Il est possible que les deux couriront une morte chaleur, or dead heat, mais je crois que Ely sera le vainqueur. Comme pour Fille de l'Air, Messieurs, elle n'a pas la fantôme d'une chance!"

Some of the French bookmakers who had laid heavy against the General, came up to NICHOLAS, and wanted to kiss the old man on the cheek; but NICHOLAS keeps his kisses for the maids of merry England—the maids of merry, merry England. Let the bottle pass, and we'll fill another glass, to the maids of merry, merry England!   NICHOLAS.

NOTE.—It will be observed that our esteemed correspondent dates " Paris, Monday, June 12," but the packet only reached us on *Friday*, June 16th, and it bore the postmark, not of Paris, but of *Windsor*. We have written to his Belgravian address for an explanation.—ED.

SERIOUS MISUNDERSTANDING BETWEEN OURSELVES AND NICHOLAS. AMPLE APOLOGY ON OUR PART. THE GOOD AND GIFTED MAN FORGIVES, AND ALL IS JOY!

Our readers have no doubt remarked the absence of any communication from NICHOLAS in our last number, but a thrill of terror, followed by a spasm of relief, will run through their breasts when we tell them that we were very near losing the invaluable services of that immortal prophet.

The following correspondence explains itself:—

1.—FROM NICHOLAS TO THE EDITOR.

BELGRAVIA.

NICHOLAS presents his compliments to the Editor, and which I have just seen Number Six of your New Serious, where it as good as hints that your Prophet was not in France at the time he made his remarkable prophecy of a dead heat between Ely and General Peel, but had waited at Ascot itself until the race was over, and then wrote a false address, a course of action as is little short of not being exactly what you would consider quite a gentlemanly thing to do, on which he will only observe that common courtesy to one almost old enough to be your grandfather, not to speak of gratitude to one whose sporting tips are equal to any in the world, bar none, and the true explanation is as follows:—That he forgot to put the letter in the post when he wrote it at the Grand Hotel, Paris, and was surprised not to hear from you in acknowledgment of its receipt, than which nothing is more clearly your duty so to do as Editor of the New Serious, and when the old man came over to England and went down to Ascot, along of many other aristocratic sportsmen, I was horrified at finding the letter still in my pocket, so posted it at Windsor along of another letter as fully explained circumstances, but which second letter it is just within the bounds of possibility as you may not have received it, NICHOLAS well remembering now that his attention is called to the fact as in his haste he forgot to stick on a Queen's head, but even then you might surely have paid the double postage if it reached you; and if to the contrary, both Reason and Equity should have forbidden to address what he can only stigmatise as a uncalled-for rebuke in public to an old man as has done a good deal to make the fortune of the New Serious, quite as much so perhaps as any of the other contributors, although than whom perchance I am sure a more affable body of young gentlemen, though a little gay.

Mr. Editor, it is *me* who have a right to an explanation, and I will say even an apology.

Withdraw your suspicions, sir, and set him right along with the Sportive Public, or not only will he contribute to other journals, but if the Prophet were not quite so much in the vale of years, or had he a son to protect him in his advanced middle age, my outraged honour might oblige me to resort to that awful measure of sending you a friend, and letting you choose your own

weapon, sir, for though old was once as fine a shot as
ever pulled a trigger at Hornsey Wood.

Yours, as you use him,

NICHOLAS.

The party who brings this Waits a responsive
answer.

II.—FROM THE EDITOR TO NICHOLAS.

80, FLEET STREET.

The Editor begs to express his regret that he has
hurt the feelings of a most esteemed contributor. He
only did so by way of joke. He unreservedly withdraws
his imputations upon the Prophet's good faith, and
humbly trusts that he may still be favoured with some
copy for Number Eight, N. S.

3.—FROM NICHOLAS TO THE EDITOR.

BELGRAVIA.

To the noblest of Editors, and one of the most
magnanimous of men.

DEAR SIR,—After your vivacious and euphemistical
epistolary composition, expressive of your contrition, in
the most valedictory and eleemosynary terms, nothing
remains for your vaticinatory prophet but cordially to
reciprocate your benevolent similes and hold forth (in
correspondence) the outstretched hand that is symbo-
lical of affectionate recognition and reconciliatory feelings of amitude and cordiality.

The heart must be greatly fuller of rancour, vindic-
tiveness, owing a grudge, evil speaking, lying or slan-
dering, than is that of NICHOLAS, which could peruse
your manly tribute without a tear of conscious rectitude
mingled with joy, and the next time he meets you hopes

as we may bury any lingering feelings of mutual animosity over a good glass of sherry wine, and should be glad if any of the other contributors would join along of us, than whom, as I have often said in the New Serious of your Sportive Organ, perhaps a more affable body of young gentlemen, though a little gay.

NICHOLAS.

I have a good thing for Goodwood, and a certainty for the Leger.

In addition to general information, will soon begin his

HISTORY OF KNURR AND SPELL ! ! !

NICHOLAS.

TOTAL FAILURE OF NICHOLAS! HIS ABSOLUTE WINNER OF THE GOODWOOD CUP SCRATCHED!! HEAVY LOSSES OF OUR PROPHET!!! GLADIATEUR!!!! GLADIATEUR!!!!! GLADIATEUR!!!!!! EXCLUSIVE TIP FOR THE ST. LEGER!!!!!!!

BELGRAVIA.

The pitcher, Mr. Editor, who goes often to the well gets broken at last, and goes to the bad. Such has been partially the fate of your own NICHOLAS. For (nearly) the first time in the Prophet's life, I have led my supporters, my good and kind supporters, the Sportive Men of England, into an error. That their losses have been less than my own is as sincere a aspiration as ever rose from a prophetic breast below.

It would be idle at this time of day, and after a catastrophe which has metaphorically stained the turf of my native land, for NICHOLAS to pretend that Gladiateur won the Goodwood Cup. NICHOLAS was present at the race, and witnessed the victory of Ely, whom he always, as you may possibly not remember, said to be a real great horse, and likely to win, especially as NICHOLAS predicted his defeat of General Peel at Ascot. Still, the Prophet sent you Gladiateur, and no kid about it, week after week.

Sir, that animal (previously selected for the Derby by NICHOLAS, when at long odds, so that if a fair average be taken you have not really lost by the old man's predictions after all) *would* have won, and *could* have won, and *should* have won, but then how *can* a horse win if scratched? All the prophets in Great Britain, than whom perchance a more delusive body of men, though pretentious, could not make it to do so.

When the news of the scratching reached his ear, NICHOLAS was so excited that he very nearly burst a vessel. When an English gentleman is verging on patriarchal periods, and has put the pot on heavy, it *is* hard to lose a great portion of the modest provision you may have made for those who are to come after.

Fortunately for NICHOLAS he had been hedging off a little, so that the blow is not so ruinous as it might have been. I shall not have to give up my house, but I shall find it absolutely necessary to insist upon an increase of wages.

MY HISTORY OF KNURR AND SPELL.

This book is in active progress. Any communications relative had better be addressed, under cover to the office, not having quite got the painters out in Belgravia, though myself returned.

NICHOLAS.

I have a good thing for the St. Leger.

THE SECOND OCTOBER MEETING, WITH ANTICIPATIONS OF THE CAMBRIDGESHIRE AT THE HOUGHTON MEETING.

BELGRAVIA.

The Newmarket Second October Meeting will have commenced before the burning words that NICHOLAS is now about to write in the MS. will be revealed to mortal eye, by being set up in type by the printer, than whom I am sure no one more attentive and obliging, though perhaps a little inclined to grumble when the old man is late with his copy. Such, the Prophet is free to own, is often the case, he being irregular in his habits of literary composition, to which he was not brought up in early life, it having more resembled a rough-and-tumble to get his bread and cheese than the pleasing studies of the Academician Grove. (Please let the printer put "Academician Grove" with a big A and a big G, it being meant as a compliment to Plato, and the printer sometimes taking upon himself to alter the Prophet's authorgraphy when such a course as to do so is not necessary.)

And so, my merry men all, under which thimble is the little pea? Salpinctes, Alabama, Privateer, Lansdown. Who is to win the Cæsarewitch? Wouldn't you like to know, my sportive readers? (Let the printer put the next part like a stage-play.)

Nicholas.—Wouldst thou?

Sportive Readers.—Yes, we wouldst, we wouldst.

Nicholas.—And who is the proper person for to give you the tip, eh, my friends and patrons? Is it the Old Man?

Sportive Readers.—Yes, we wouldst, leastways of course we mean, Yes, it is! NICHOLAS is him!

Nicholas.—Am I right?

Sportive Readers.—Yes, we wouldst ! Give us the tip.

Nicholas.--Wait a minute, you dear impatient creatures. Who was it that sent you Gladiateur for the Derby ?

Sportive Readers.—It was NICHOLAS.

Nicholas.—Who was the only Prophet in the land, bar none, who foretold a dead heat at Ascot between Ely and General Peel, with the former to win at the second try ?

Sportive Readers.—Come now, NICHOLAS, *that's* pitching it a little *too* strong, *that* is. You *might* have foretold it ; but you told us yourself that you forgot to post the letter containing the prediction, which in consequence never saw the light until after the race. No, NICHOLAS, stick to facts. Facts will speak trumpet-tongued in your favour, you good and gifted aged man. Never will it be forgotten whilst a single annal of the British turf remains, how gloriously you vaticinated the absolute winner of the St. Leger ; only don't exaggerate.

Nicholas.—You are right, my worthy friends. The old man spoke from memory, which is apt to fail one at his period, but in future will always refer to his notes, and is proud and pleased to find you anxious for his tip about the Cæsarewitch. Thinking that you would probably like a clear and definite selection, naming first, second, and third.

Sportive Readers.—So we wouldst. Old man, you are correct.

Nicholas.—Thinking such, the Prophet has sent a private note to the Editor, than whom a more affable gentleman, though a little averse to raising NICHOLAS' weekly wages, asking him to arrange to have a

SPECIAL NUMBER OF FUN.

In this number I pledge myself to name

FIRST, SECOND, AND THIRD, IN THE CÆSAREWITCH.

Sportive Readers.—Well, then, our trusty guide, wouldst thou not partake of some refreshment, say a bottle of sherry wine?

Nicholas.—Yes, I wouldst—at least, no—don't print *that*, mind, because it looks undignified, and too colloquial, and might give the mistaken impression that the Prophet was a regular old sot, but put it down like this, more: No, I wouldst *not! After* my prophecy have appeared, *after* my selection have won, the old man will gladly celebrate the festive and emolumentary occasion in the flowing bowl, but not before, such being unbecoming of a Sportive Editor of the New Serious, and now, to show that refusal of your hospitality is not prompted by ingratitude, let me give you in addition

A FEW NOTES ON THE CAMBRIDGESHIRE,

A hippic contest which will not take place before the 24th, so that I shall have plenty of time to keep you posted up, and to-day will speak cursory.

NICHOLAS.

FAILURE OF GLADIATEUR. THE PROPHET UNDER A CLOUD AND A NEW ASPECT.

BERMONDSEY.

REVERED AND HONOURED EDITOR,—It is of no use attempting to deceive *you*, Sir, and the old man will not try such. Sir, he has lost enormous!

The sex has always been peculiar fatal to NICHOLAS, and, figuratively speaking, it is again a woman's hand that deals the avenging blow, alluding, of course, to Garde-visure, the mare that won the Cambridgeshire on Tuesday fortnight. You may have noticed he was absent from your columns in Numbers 24 and 25; in fact, I have a rather harsh and vituperatory letter from you to that effect;[1] but, Sir, revered and honoured Mr. Editor,[2] the fact is, the Prophet was out of town, and up to his old games. What's bred in the bone, Sir, will come out in the flesh; and despite his ample recent means, when once you've been a tout, a tout you'll ever be; and he was hanging about the stables just as in the old days; and the cold getting into his head, not to speak of whiskey and water affecting him more than it did before he generally could partake of sherry-wine when he liked, the old man, Sir, overslept hisself,[3] and was too ill to send his usual countrybution.

I wouldst, Sir, that this were the worst! But no! the Star of NICHOLAS have set, perhaps to raise no more; and Newmarket Heath has been his Waterloo, not from the point of view of the late occupant of Apsley House, but more Napoleonic in its character.

It is easy to say, after the event, "Why did you go and do so, oh NICHOLAS, you good but fond old man?" Why? Because I had a blind faith in a noble animal; because Jennings himself said, "He'll do it, Mister N., if they was to put a Pickford's wan on the top of him!" because the Count de Lagrange said, with his own lips, "*Courage, mong voo!*" Sir, my belief in Gladiateur was almost idolatryastical! It was vainly they told me he *couldn't* do it with 9 stone 12; your NICHOLAS put the pot on heavy, and is now, speaking comparative, an abject pauper and a broken-hearted, ruinous old man! It's lucky for me as I've no one to come after me, in the way of children at least (there are a good many after me in another way), former allusions to olive-branches having only been hypothetic and good-humourous.

Do you remember—very likely not, for you know no more than a babe just unborn about sportive matters,[4] though the best of editors, and the most indulgent of masters I am sure—*do* you remember the odds that were laid against the winning mare Gardevisure ? They were 33 to 1.

Murder will out. *They were laid by* Nicholas!

There. I feel easier in my mind after the confession. Ruin (again speaking comparative) stares me in the face with a vulgarity of aspect to which the contemptuous expression of unpaid landladies in former years was Rimmel's fountain to a rotten egg; the colossal edifice of Prophetic Wealth is rudely shaken by the breeze of adverse fortune; but this emotion unbecomes a Nicholas, who, if he have known better days, have also known worse, and was never ashamed of *honest* Poverty,[5] whatever may be said by the pens of the detractorial.

I have thought it quite as well not to go back to Belgravia just at present. The fact is, that a little seclusion will do me no harm, so shall lie by and try to pull it off over the Liverpool Cup. He has always borne a honest name, praise be; and if the worst comes to the worst, he has still his abilities as a public writer to fall back upon. Mrs. Cripps, the landlady, has got me a life of Sir Walter Scott, Baronet, from the circulating library round the corner, and it almost brings the tears into a poor ruinous old Prophet's eyes— thankye, Mrs. Cripps, yes ; a little more sugar in it this time, please![6]—to read how that good and great man

3

paid off his debts by his novels. And will write one himself against any Prophet of his age or size bar none! Well, well, it's a long lane that's got no turning; and what says the classic bard, as I heard him quoted by an affable young gent from Cambridge College on the Heath itself?—

How d'ye? my eye! Crass Tibby![7]

Thanks, much, my dear Mrs. Cripps. If the offer of a old man's heart and hand[8]—where the deuce is Mrs. Cripps? Shall make up to old gal, hang *me* if I don't. My clothes is all right; and still I looks the cynicsure of fashion with my light autumnal overcoat;[9] and I say, Mrs. Fun—Cripps I mean—if a old man's honest hadoration, if a fond heart's gentle throb, if—oh, I say, old boy, of course you won't print this, which is purely confidential—can't write any more to-night—sight's not what it was, you know—only I was a-thinking, Sir, you might have it put in large type as I sent you GARDEVISURE FOR ABSOLUTE WINNER, only you was out of town, and so such never saw the light;[10] but anyhow you'll not desert the old one in his adversity? You'll keep him on, noble Captain, as your Sportive Editor? Eh? Thankye; there's a dear good soul, Mrs. Cripps! If a old man's fervent—but will now conclude.

So no more at present from, yours,
THE RUINOUS NICHOLAS.

EDITORIAL NOTES.

[1] We simply gave expression to a very natural feeling of annoyance.

[2] This servile adulation will do NICHOLAS no good.

³ The old man ought to have known better.

⁴ Don't you be too sure of that, old man!

⁵ Perhaps because he never tried it.

⁶ Oh, NICHOLAS, NICHOLAS, at it again!

⁷ Is it possible the Prophet means "Hodie mihi, cras tibi?"

⁸ We had no idea the old man was so susceptible.

⁹ "Vanity-glorious" again.

¹⁰ We utterly repudiate this disgraceful suggestion.

BERMONDSEY.

REVERED AND HONOURED SIR,—When a man has
arrived at the period of NICHOLAS he is not over likely
to take a sanguineous and enthusiastical view of human
nature; but never you believe, Mr. Editor, what the
cynic would tell you with regard to the innate depravity
of the mortal heart. It is only when a man is really
down upon his luck that he knows how much good
nature and benevolence is possessed by those around
him, a conspicuous instance of such having been your
generous insertion last week of my countrybution at
enormous length at a time when my literary earnings
are almost the only emolumentary resources which a
ruinous old man can metaphorically fall back upon,
although he considers that some of your editorial com-
mentations, however well meant, were less calculated
to convey the idea of your regarding him in the light
of Age and Virtue under a temporary cloud of adversity than of one who was rather a disreputable old
tout.

Your Prophet has likewise to acknowledge the ex-
treme kindness of his temporary landlady, Mrs. Cripps,
than whom I am sure a more amiable person, though,
perhaps, a little middle-aged; and remarkable, indeed,

have been the increased kindness since the appearance
of your paper where she was put in print, she having
been previously rather distrustful whether NICHOLAS
was indeed the eminent man he represented, but on
seeing him to be really your Sportive Editor, and as
such in the possession of a moderate but certain in-
come, immediately came up-stairs to inquire whether
the Prophet would object to such a thing being offered
as a few shrimps for a relish to his tea, and very nice
they were.   Yes, Sir, woman's heart is indeed a well-
spring of affection; and I send you a slight instalment
of a poem on the subject in emulation of the " Elegy
in a Country Churchyard."   I call it an "Elegy in a
Bermondsey Parlour," and the first line must be understood as purely figurative, taking such a liberty in real
life being what NICHOLAS would never dream of doing
so if sober :—

> " Here rests his head upon the lap of Cripps,
>   A Prophet who to Fun was well beknown ;
> But Fortune frowned on his autumnal tips,
>   And Garderisure marked him for her own."

And may send you other specimens of what he will
venture to invoke as the Eligiac Mews.

But if you, Sir, have been more than kind, and if
Mrs. Cripps be all my fancy painted her, only in still
more roseate hues, how different has been the treatment
he receives from many who ought to have known better !

Never until Michaelmas had your Prophet been
behind hand with the rent for his Belgravian mansion,
and to all his servants he was really benevolent.   And
yet, Sir, what were the expressions of the landlord
when told that NICHOLAS must relinquish his palatial
abode, and would be glad of a little time to make up

the quarter's rent? Sir, he said, "I am glad to get rid of you at any price, and to free my house from the incubus of a notorious betting-man, who has at length met with the proper fate of his disgraceful avocations;" and this, Sir, after many is the glass of sherry wine that he has partook at my expense!

This is not the only indignity your NICHOLAS has had to endure. His valet, meeting him promiscuous at a public I use, absolutely turned up his purse-proud nose at one who had seen better days, and spoke of him to the landlady as "a low reporter;" but I remembered the dignity of Literature, Sir, as one entrusted with your confidence, and bearing likewise in mind the period at which I have arrived, NICHOLAS forebore to smite the arrogant menial to the earth, and being a very nicely sanded floor, and only regarded him with a contumelious expression to which the glare of the angriest basilisk is a gentle glance of connubial affection. And then, Sir, leaving the house and paying my score with a conscious dignity of a honest though a ruinous old man, I wended my way to *another* establishment, where a man is still treated *as* a man in spite of unmerited pecuniary affliction, and washed away the memory of the insult in a glass of something warm.

A few of my friends are talking of "A NICHOLAS TESTIMONIAL," in recognition of his services to the Turf. You may possibly remember, Sir—not that *you* know much about sportive matters, nor ever did, though the ablest of editors and the best of friends—that a similar compliment was recently paid to Admiral Rous.

NICHOLAS.

I have a good thing for next year's Derby.

"When things are at the worst they're sure to mend," is a saying in respect of which NICHOLAS will only assert that, supposing such to be true, now is the time for them to do so. A splendid opportunity now presents itself to Fortune's revolving wheel, and no flies; and if life is but a seesaw I object to the present situation of my end of the plank. What says the Poet? Why he says, does that gifted writer whom I do not remember his name, that " A sorrow's crown of sorrows is remembering happier things." *That's* where it is, Sir; *that's* where the shoe pinches; *that's* where a poor and ruinous old man really finds out that his corns are hurting of him. I *have* "a sorrow's crown of sorrows," and it's pretty nearly the only crown I have, or even half such. "What then?" it may be asked by the individuous and the proud, which many is the contumelious upstart as once gladly partook of sherry wine at the old man's expense, though now exulting over the fallen trunk of the monarch of the forest glade, speaking metaphorical. "What then? NICHOLAS, you forlorn and abandoned old tout, this ain't the first time you've been down upon your luck. You're *used* to it, *you* are, you fond and talkative old tipster!"

Talkative he may be, and a tipster he is; nor will NICHOLAS deny that he *have* often been down upon his luck, more's the pity; but it all depends upon your condition previous, and the height from which you fall. It is one thing to fall off of a easy chair, but quite another guess sort of matter to be hurled impetuous from the topmost summit of Himalaya's snowy peak. When the Prophet was in comparatively humble life— though an honester elderly man never took in *Ruff's*

Guide to the Turf—a run of bad luck simply meant restricting of himself in a few of his little comforts, and keeping carefully out of the way until it should blow over; but since then, Sir, NICHOLAS had risen by his own unaided talent to a pedestal of prosperity quite palatial in its character; and at my period it *is* hard to have to begin the world again, there being more competition than ever, and to shrink from the Belgravian magnate dispensing of elegant refreshment to the good and great on a scale of profusion combined with every delicacy of the season and sherry wine, down to the humble inmate of a low Bermondsey lodging-house, though no offence is intended to Mrs. Cripps, than whom a kinder nor a better woman, though a little looking after her rent.

Many of my Job's comforters say—and goodness knows advice is cheap—"Why don't you take a hair of the dog that bit you? You suffered through blind confidence in a noble but over-weighted animal. Never mind; have another shy; fling in your old castor to the ring once more, and put the pot on!"

How can I?

Sir, the racing season is over !

Literary labour, Mr. Editor, must to NICHOLAS be that sheet-anchor of prosperity which, though often nipped in the bud, ultimately unfurls its wings upon a prouder pedestal than ever! And he will accordingly commence as soon as possible his Review of the Sportive Season of 1865, as well as his

HISTORY OF KNURR AND SPELL.

NICHOLAS.

P.S.—I have a good thing for next year's Derby.

P.S. No. 2.—Do you not think, Sir, that the time have now arrived for raising of the Prophet's salary? The winter is likely to be a hard one; beef is at a shilling per pound; and though Mrs. Cripps is goodness itself, she rather prefers being paid the rent at regular intervals to being told that it will be all right in a day or two, though temporary ill-convenient to settle, and once so far forget herself as to denominate him, when he tried to pacify her with a joke, as a superannuated old buffoon.

NICHOLAS ON THE FESTIVE SEASON.

BERMONDSEY.

The Prophet begs to thank Mr. Editor for graciously inserting his little poetical card in reference to the Christmas party at NICHOLAS' own happy two pair back. A contented mind is a continual feast, and though he could only offer M. Jean Godin, which was the one gentleman of all your once-affable staff, that accepted the invitation, a hermit's fare, as all will admit a piece of roast beef to consist of, on such an occasion, yet the party went off with great éclaw, one of NICHOLAS' own family having recognized me at last and took me up, and he being himself quite a merchant prince in the general grocery and was once on the very brink of becoming a churchwarden, may yet resume my position and cut a dash in civic society, such being based on a prouder pinnacle of commercial prosperity than the gilded saloons of an effeminate aristocracy which was once hand and glove with the old man and only too eager to get on his selections for coming events. He fell; Fortune, that fickle jade, deserted him; and of all who once put their legs under the Prophet's mahogany in Belgravia, from your own other contributors (than whom I am sure) down to peers of the realm, not one has found him out in his Bermondsey retreat. Ah, such is life, but luck may take a turn—and if my cousin should continue to take me up, as I hope for the best, and the Derby selection turn out prophetically inspired, you will all of you be glad enough to rally around me again, with your "Well, MR. NICHOLAS, here's your good health, Sir, in a glass of sherry wine." I know the world; I know it to be as hollow as a race that is sold; —but I bear no malicious rankerings in my bosom, and I wish you all a much happier New Year and many more of them than it is the Prophet's candid opinion you really deserve.

Luck *has* turned; I always knew it would; and I trust I shall know how to conduct myself in restored affluence when it comes to pass, *as it will*, as well as I did when the bitter blasts of pecuniary adversity had swept me from my pinnacle and blew derisively around my prophetic head.   NICHOLAS.

I have a good thing for this year's Derby.

PECKHAM.

MR. NICHOLAS presents his very friendly and quite cordial compliments to the Editor of *Fun*, whose missive (if an exceedingly uncalled for and peremptorial and individuous note, not even sealed with wax, but in a mere gummed envelope like the lowest of the low) did not reach him at those temporal premises in Bermondsey which shielded for a time your Prophet's hoary head against the pelting of pitiless impecuniosity, not to speak of many who would have gladly locked me up.

The best thanks of MR. NICHOLAS are due to that very worthy person Mrs. Cripps, who forwarded the note to the house where the Prophet now resides, the honoured guest of a relation who has took him up.

MR. NICHOLAS has known the lap of prosperity and he has, if he may be allowed the expression, often curled himself up like a dog on the doorstep of adversity. But he is now basking in the mild halo of the middle classes —a halo that only blooms once in a hundred years sixty of which he can vouch for as being within his period.

The epithets " Come, old man, put your best foot foremost, we want your Derby selection, and the printers are waiting for your history of Knurr and Spell," may not have been intended as contumelious nor designed to bring a tear ; but it was in very different terms, Sir, that you were once wont to address him ; and he will gladly suppose you wrote such after dinner, the caliph-gravy being of a shambling sort, and youth will be served. The Prophet is far too mature a sportive cove to grudge any one his fling, but it will not mitigate your dying hour to remember that you heaped the more casual and promiscuous ashes on a timeworn heart bowed down.

Thanks to my relative and his commercial ante-cedents, the Prophet now wants for nothing, but will gladly continue his flirtation with the Mewses in the columns of your New Serious, and hopes henceforward to be able to devote more leisure to the purely literary portion of his task, having endeavoured to form a good English style by devoting of his days and nights to the study of the Daily Press.

THE SPORTIVE KALENDER FOR 1866.

JANUARY.

January—so called from "JANE," a domestic, and "airey" her Paphian bower—is adapted rather for the youthful sportsman, always a good deal after the manner of a fool, and committing excesses which have afterwards to be atoned for by stethoscopes and post-mortems,—than for a mature cove, who, if in affluence, will very properly stop at home with a glass of something warm and the columns of the Daily Press, Britain's Palladium.

SKATING.—Nothing can be more seasonable, and he was once as fond of it as angling, but at a certain period you would much rather be safe at home with the columns of the Daily Press, that fourth estate, and a glass of something warm.

SWIMMING.—I have wrote this down because desired by my relative who once won a silver cup. But you don't find your Prophet trying to do so.

NICHOLAS.

PECKHAM.

Literary pursuits, however delightful, are not perhaps quite so attractive when a Prophet is basking in the lapse of luxury as when your poor old man is comparatively speaking down upon his luck. From the time when a weekly remittance ceases to be like the liberty of the press and the air we breathe—which, if we have such not, we die—from the time when the bounty of a relative in return for private tips given in advance have soothed the path of honest and middle-aged toil,—from that instant, Mr. Editor, a Prophet is apt to be irregular in sending of his copy into you. Not to attempt deceptive treatment of one whose character I admire, he having always paid me on the nail for work done, NICHOLAS will plainly confess that he has been living, so to speak, in clover, and wallowing in refined enjoyments, such as a quiet evening with a little music, to which he had long been comparative a stranger. The Prophet, Sir, has not wasted his time; he and his august Relative, than whom I am sure a better man never drew the breath of retail trade, though a little apt to have forgotten NICHOLAS' existence until he heard, trumpet-tongued, of his literary fame—both of us, Mr. Editor, have *made our books*. EARLY. They may be subject to modifications. Post betting is all very well; but it wouldn't suit a Prophet to encourage such.

The *Sheffield Independent*, Mr. Editor, is a paper which NICHOLAS esteems, with which is incorporated admiration; but when he wrote as follows, on the 10th of February this annum, oh, why did not his heart misgive him?—

"GEORGE MOSFORTH, OF SHIRE GREEN, FORKMAKER, v. WILLIAM CUTTS THE YOUNGER, OF ECCLESFIELD, FILE CUTTER.—In this case, Mr. Binney, jun., was for the plaintiff, and Mr. Chambers was for the defendant. The action was brought to recover 40s., balance of a sum of 50s. deposited with the defendant, as stake-holder on a game of knurr and spell—a peculiar game, of which an exposition has been promised in FUN at different times for two years past, on the supposition that it is one of those things that no fellow can be expected to understand; and the comic sporting contributor has himself acted on this supposition, for we believe the exposition has never been given. This particular game was played between the two men named Ospring and Brown, but the referee was dissatisfied, or aggrieved, and left the ground. The plaintiff, therefore, now sought to recover his stake, on the ground that the match had not been fulfilled. Mr. Chambers, however, upset this plea, and his honour gave judgment for the defendant, but without costs."

Sir, part of this is true. I admit, in the largest capitals you like.

MY HISTORY OF KNURR AND SPELL HAVE NOT YET APPEARED.

No, Sir; *nor will it* if I am thus subjected to intimidation, arising (no doubt) from a very excusable feeling of disappointment.

A work, Mr. Editor, like my " Knurr and Spell " or Gibboon's " Decline and Fall " is the fruit of patient researches and of classic lore. NICHOLAS may be led, Sir, but he won't be drove. He is at present collecting of his materials, perhaps nearer Sheffield than the Editor of the *Independent* is aware; ha, ha, thou provincial contemporary!

But NICHOLAS is sure that the notice is kindly meant though a little gay. If I thought otherwise, old as I am, would fight him now, catch-weight, for fifty pound aside, if my Relative behaved as I think he would.

Or, secondly, *I will play him at the game itself*, and you, Sir, shall be umpire, if you are quite sure that you know enough about the rules to enable you to see fair!

NICHOLAS.

P.S. (1).—I have a good thing for the Derby.

P.S. (2).—In active preparation, and will shortly be produced,

A HISTORY OF KNURR AND SPELL.

Anticipations of the Derby, and Prophecy for the University Boat Race.

PECKHAM.

The poet Campbell, than whom I am sure a more energetic bard though a little less generally read than he used to be, has remarked that

> " 'Tis the sunset of life gives us mystical lore,
> And coming events cast their shadows afore!"

Such are my own sentiments, although the old man is still worth half-a-dozen sunsets any day in the week. This period, however, is that which is alluded to casual by another bard to the effect that

> " Old experience did attain
> To something like prophetic strain."

The "prophetic strain" of NICHOLAS *is* "something like!"

In this, the First Number of the Third Volume of the New Series, the Prophet will take a comprehensive glance (like a bird) over the sportive world, and tell you what I see there. If you like, Sir, you can put it in the form of a Vision, and calling of it

THE PROPHET'S DREAM.

I.

Ha! ha!

I see a multitude, a mighty multitude—ever so many coves, in point of fact, from Britannia's Hope and Cambria's Pride, riding on horseback and smoking of a princely Havanuah, down to the promiscuous Welsher and the casual tout.

I see a broad and open heath, truly spacious, and affording an eligible opportunity for the favourite old English sport of running the Derby next May.

The Prophet's gaze stretches far and wide. I see them—at last! They're off!

Who has Won?

The Prophet's gaze suddenly becomes cloudy and obscure, as if NICHOLAS had had too much to drink over night, though goodness knows, it was only a casual glass of sherry wine, and stood him by a relative, for the matter of that.

Who are the First Three?

The Prophet's gaze cannot tell you at present, my noble sportsmen; but would only advise you not to put your money on Lord Lyon.

II.

Ha! ha!

I see a multitude, a mighty multitude—ever so many coves, in point of fact, from Britannia's Hope and Cambria's Pride, standing on the paddle-box and smoking of a princely Havannah, down to the promiscuous stoker and the low bargee.

I see the noble river, Father Thames.

Hail to the Prophet's gaze, ye noble Father Thames! Ha! ha!

These are the children of Cambridge, that splendid old Alma Mater, at which NICHOLAS did not receive the greater portion of his early education.

Yonder sit the sons of Oxford, a famous University to which the same personal remark applies.

They're off! The Prophet shouts like a good 'un. It is a glorious struggle! Well rowed, thou plucky Cantabs! Bravo, thou strong Oxonians!

Who has Won?

Wouldst ye know, thou sportive public? Then gaze upon the rosette worn by NICHOLAS *after* the race, one of two which he brought down with him so as to be prepared for whatever might happen! Gaze upon that rosette, and ye know the winner.

III.

Ha! ha!

I see a multitude, a mighty multitude—ever so many coves, in point of fact, but Britannia's Hope and Cambria's Pride is *not* present, and (accordingly) is *not* smoking of a princely Havannah. In fact, take it as a whole, the crowd is rather a low one than principally composed of men of rank and title.

Wouldst thou know what mysterious purpose has brought them hither?

" We wouldst," ye answer. Listen to your NICHOLAS. Perhaps you think it is the fight between Mace and Goss? Perhaps you would like a tip?

No, thou credulous subscribers!

Look at yonder couple! *'Tis they!*

The Prophet's gaze outvies that of the ordinary eagle as he bends his glittering orbs upon a public place in the neighbourhood of Sheffield, and marks the merry sport.

THEY ARE PLAYING AT KNURR AND SPELL.

Ha! ha! NICHOLAS.

I have a good thing for the Two Thousand.

OUR PROPHECY FOR THE BOAT RACE.

PUTNEY.

With a fidelity to the interests of your paper as a sportive organ only equalled by that of the domestic needle to the pole, the Prophet has temporary left his snug abode in Peckham, and taken up his quarters in lodgings at this place, which as you are well aware of, is situated on the banks of the Thames. And here will NICHOLAS remain, with the exception of an occasional run up to town, just to look in at Tattersall's, and lay the odds with a duke or two, until the great contest of next Saturday is over.

It cannot be truthfully stated that your old man was ever much of an aquatical celebrity, he having always fought rather shy of cold water, and once when rowing in a wherry with a young woman, who afterwards threw him over at the last moment, was run down by a racing gig, which long had a tendency to envenomize his mind against boating in general. Such prejudice may have been subsequentially removed, but it is necessarily still dormant in my mind at my period of life.

Nor has NICHOLAS generally been fortunate in his adventures at the race itself. No later than last year when I was talking perfectly affable to a young marchioness as I know, the Prophet was upset into the stream ignominiously by the tow-rope of a barge, so that NICHOLAS had to go home and change his trousers, besides being chivied as an old guy.

Nevertheless, Mr. Editor, on behalf of your paper and of the sportive public—by which he does not mean a pugilistical tavern, but the athletic men of merry, merry England, chorus,—NICHOLAS has again exposed himself to the perils of the deep, and in your next impression will give the name of the absolute winner, together with a minute account, graphic, personal, and a little gay, of the race itself. What is really wanted of him, however, at the present moment is no doubt a prophecy, and such he will now make.

Cambridge are better than last year; but so are Oxford.

Superstitious people will tell you that luck will have a turn. Your Prophet says No!

With the kindliest feelings towards the manly Cantabonians, NICHOLAS is still bound to wear

THE OLD DARK BLUE,

and to place them as follows :—

Oxford 1
Cambridge 2

> Friday-night, the Twenty-third—it *is* the Twenty-third isn't it ?—well, I don't know after twelve o'clock— I should rather think it was, too, old fellow ! Twenty-fourth and say no more about it. Shixty-shix.

The amicable contest between the sister Universities, than whom I am sure none more respectable though a little gay, of the Isis and the Cam, has long been felt deeply interesting by all who were deeply interested in the amicable contest between the sister Universities of the Isis and the Cam ; and a party of distinguished students from the banks of both the Isis *and* the Cam, knowing the Prophet's period of life, and anxious to keep me square for to-morrow—no, this *is* to-morrow— anxious as they were yesterday to keep me square, last night and this cold, chilly morning have steadily been plying NICHOLAS with the most delicious—*delicious*— with the most delicious evervexing drinks, gentlemen, that the Prophet has ever tasted from the banks of either the Isis *or* the Cam—I say, gentlemen, *or* the Cam, in their amicable contest which has long been felt so deeply interesting on the sister shores of the Isis *and* the Cam. Not another drop—will do his duty to his Editor to the last—well, if I *must*, let it be a little brandy hot with........ Gentlemen, gentle—*men*, we shall have a long ride of it from here to Putlake.........And gentlemen,—don't go !—we shall be safe to want some more refreshment at Mortney, when the crews—bless 'em both !—have rowed up from Putlake—*don't* go, yet !—stand by the old man—will do his duty to his Editor to the last in the amicable contest between the Isis *against* the Cam !.........I slay the Prophet's got—good thing—Derby. P.S.—Knurr and Spell.

Saturday Morning.

Further P.S.—Oxford won—Cambridge two.

Triumphant Success of Nicholas ! Successful Triumph of the Prophet !! Nicholas Right Again ! ! ! Nicholas Named the Absolute First and Second in the University Race ! ! ! ! The Prophet's Profits ! ! ! ! ! Disgraceful Practical Joke upon the Editor ! ! ! ! ! !

Peckham.

Mr. Editor,—Where are we now, sir ? Upon what kind of pinnacle do you imagine that your Prophet is now asserting of his proud pre-eminence as a Sportive organ ? Was there any doubt about his vaticinations *this* time ? Did he use mysterious and ambiguical terms, concealing his meaning behind half Johnson's Dixouary ?

No, sir, he did *not* ! Long before the race, he selected the crew on which he felt disposed to pitch his prophetic fancy ; and his absolute prophecy, *vide* your own columns in the New Serious for the week before the race, was,

Oxford 1

Cambridge 2

Well, sir, and what was the actual bona-fide result ?

Oxford Eight 1

Cambridge Eight.......................... 2

Chiswick Ait 0

The Prophet is bound to confess that, not being exactly quite so much of an aquatical authority as when he takes his stand upon his native turf, and his name is NICHOLAS; he was not himself aware, previous to the morning of the race, that Chiswick was engaged in it; nor did he recognize, speaking personally, any boat of that description; but as the Chiswick Ait is frequently referred to by rowing men, I will not rob a poor village of its due, though unsuccessful.

After so complete a triumph, it goes against the heart of a man, especially at NICHOLAS's period, to complain of anything that may wear the complexion of individuality or blame; but the Prophet, sir, is bound to say that you were grossly imposed upon, and ought to have exercised greater editorial care, when you printed, as though it came from NICHOLAS's own hand, a portion of my last impression, which would lead to the idea that the Prophet were the worse for drink. Those who know his character would not believe such ; but it might, nevertheless, have injured him with the majority of the British public, than whom I am sure a greater fool, though a little inclined to be bumptious.

I allude, sir, to that portion of my graphic and descriptive report which is supposed to have been written on the night before the race, and which I am sure anybody, to look at a good deal of its authorgraphy might fairly suppose NICHOLAS to be either grossly illiterative or else shockingly mops and brooms, but the honest truth, Mr. Editor, is that whilst the sentiments and opinions and general style are those of the Prophet, and of which he is justly proud, the blunders are those of a young Oxford man which wrote it down from my own lips, but the champagne, he being rather a feeble sort of young fellow though generous as the day, had affected his authorgraphy, and I have often noticed that whilst they may be very good at heathenish classicals, University men can't hold a candle as concerns English grammar compared with them what has been educated in more modern academies and picked it up according.

One thing the Prophet is resolved upon after this unfortunate accident: never again will NICHOLAS submit to dictation.

You will be glad to hear, and so I am sure will the athletic men of merry, merry England, that NICHOLAS put the pot on heavy; and if similarly successful on the other great events may look forward, without arrogance, to a speedy return to those Belgravian saloons which he adorned but got tired of.

NICHOLAS.

P.S.—Shortly will be published, uniform with "Rous on Racing," only racier, "Knurr and Spell: a History." Give your orders early.

He cuts the following from his esteemed contemporary, *The Sporting Life*, than whom a more vivacious and well-informed periodical for the money, though a little gay :—

> " KNURR AND SPELL.— CUTTS AND OXSPRING.—This match has resulted in each man drawing his own money."

Of course! Any one familiar with the game might have foreseen such a result from the beginning. The Prophet's own work on the subject (illustrated by graphotype) is in active preparation.

THE RACE FOR THE GUINEAS! SINGULAR TRIUMPH OF NICHOLAS!! THE OLD MAN NAMED THE ABSOLUTE LAST FOR THE TWO THOUSAND!!! SUBSCRIBERS, HE SENT YOU OXFORD FOR THE BOAT RACE!!!! THE PROPHET GIVES A TIP FOR THE CHESTER CUP!!!!! WHO IS THE ONLY SAFE ADVISER?????? NICHOLAS, NICHOLAS!!!!!!!

PECKHAM.

The Prophet, whose candour is not inferior to his courage—indeed, it has been often remarked individuously that they are much of a muchness, meaning thereby to convey the idea that he possesses very little of either—is not going to try to humbug an intelligent editor by saying that he *positively* foretold Lord Lyon as the *absolute* winner of the Two Thou. Quite the contrary. Despite the public form of that good and gifted horse, NICHOLAS said, " Don't you back him, sir!" and accordingly a leaf from the Prophet's chaplet may be said at present to resemble more closely a piece of rotten cabbage than anything in the laurel line. Your old man, sir, has done enough—he has sufficiently established his world-wide reputation amongst the athletic men of merry, merry England—to enable him to confess a failure—*when* he fails!

But, sir and subscribers, *did* he fail? Was his failure complete in its totality? or, rather, was he not the happy instrument of sending you and your readers, than whom I am sure, advice which was literally worth more than its weight in gold? Let us see.

So long ago as April, the Prophet put you all on your guard against one of the most notorious imposters (subsequentially proved) in the race. (*In* the race, indeed! He never *was* in it! Parenthesis. Now go on, Messrs. Printers and Co., as if nothing had happened). In the place referred to, you will find these prophetic warnings :—

"NICHOLAS NEVER PROPHESIED STUDENT!"

It gives a thrill of honest joy, sir, to a bosom at my period, when I reflect that this seasonable caution may have saved many a young and ardent spirit (by which nothing liquorish is meant) from ruination.

Yet, was even this the *only* service rendered by one whom nothing but a feeling of proper pride compels me not to allow to be nameless? No. Why, sir, in the very latest number, NICHOLAS thus described a private trial of the French horse—print straight on, same as this, the extract being too long for capitals—after describing, in a few brief but graphic touches, the scene of the trial, and the appearance of a mysterious figure, NICHOLAS says, "Welcome, ye Count de Lagrange, proprietor of the sweetest animal the Prophet ever backed" (such meaning Gladiateur, whose name will ever be imperishably associated with my own appellation). "Look—Auguste is tried, Auguste is found wanting."

Thus, sir, I wrote; for thus was the prophetic afflatus stirring me.

And what, sir, was the result? I quote from the contemporaneous chroniclers of sport: "The last of all was Auguste, who pulled up very lame."

On the whole, therefore, his tip was tolerably successful by way of warning young men against vicious speculations, which are sure to lead them to ruin in the long run; and although it is quite true that I did not send you the absolute first, nevertheless remember always that

NICHOLAS SENT YOU THE ABSOLUTE LAST!

*   *   *   *   *

NICHOLAS.

PECKHAM.

Subscribers all, and ye, Mr. Editor, the old man gives you joy! Once more has the sagacity of NICHOLAS been vindicated by the event; once more, if you have all been faithful to his tips, and put the pot on heavy, ye must have cleared enormous sums.

Whilst other vaticinators went wool-gathering after Delight and Baragah, both of which broke down disastrous, what did NICHOLAS send you? It is true that he did not name Dalby as the positive first, but he gave you two to select from, and what was

THE SECOND IN HIS PROPHECY? REDCAP!

Very good, he can say no fairer than such; but permit him to put another question. What was

THE SECOND IN THE RACE? REDCAP!!

Facts like these, Mr. Editor, speak trumpet-tongued; or, if such an illustration may be allowed, like a whole brass band, in favour of your Sportive Editor, clearly proving his sapiency and worth.

Subscribers, I feel that I am again in my old form, and trust you will remit the Prophet liberal out of winnings.

There was a time when he was temporary under a cloud, like many other eminent characters have been so, such as Napoleon at Caprera, and Garibaldi at St. Helena; but what, after all, is life, sir, except a succession of see-saws, by which I do not mean maritime proverbs, but upses and downses?

Wealth may vanish, and the occupant of abodes truly palatial may be driven to a parlour at Mrs. Cripp's in Bermondsey; station may be matable; but I will freely tell you, Mr. Editor, what it is which is superior to the vacillations of Fortune and Change. It is GENIUS, Mr. Editor; it is that sacred spark which you will find freely scattered up and down my writings, and which have made me a Household Word. With Genius, and really good information from the chief training quarters, which it is always the Prophet's object to procure—with such qualities, sir, an honest man may say with the poet,

" And mistress of herself though China fall !"

But will now pass on to fresh fields and pastors new.

NICHOLAS.

THE VISION OF NICHOLAS.

PECKHAM.

No sooner, Mr. Editor, did the old man receive your somewhat peremptory orders to be prophetical and visionary than he made ready for such a course, although under difficulties. To tell the honest truth, the vision of NICHOLAS is no longer what it was except with the aid of glasses, though, thanks be, he is not yet in such a condition as poor old Homer, better known perhaps as

" The blind old bird of Sigh-oh's rocky aisle! "

Feelings of anxiety, Sir, mingle with those of pride when the prophet is informed that you are going to publish my portrait. If it is faithful I care not who sees it, though free to admit that at one period of my prophetical career I was averse from anything which might lead to my personal identification, many a backer having sworn to break every bone in that "rascally old tout's" body, meaning NICHOLAS's. Your artises will, I am sure, do their best for the old man, and if the gentleman who draws it should give satisfaction and Fortune smile on my tip, will be ready to meet him over a friendly glass of sherry wine.

With regard to "any suggestions I may have to offer," as you kindly state, do you not think, Sir, that the nose of NICHOLAS ought to be a little toned-down in a pictorial drawing of that organ? The old man hopes that he is not vanity-glorious, though considered far from bad-looking in his palmy zenith; but a nose, Sir, especially when exposed a good deal to the weather, is scarcely one of those things that can be improved by keeping; and the ruddy hue which is considered the emblem of innocence on a maiden's cheek, might be mistaken on a prophet's nose for the result of systematic inebriety. Then, Sir, you might give the artis a hint about the old man's dress, brushing him up a bit, so to speak, and making him look spruce. If these little matters are attended to, I have no doubt but what the picture will be worthy of Raffles, or even of those early Greeks (one of whom I take to be of Welsh extraction by his name, Greeks and Welshers going well together), Ap Ellis and Zookses.

These remarks perhaps need not be printed, as, if you suppress them, it will tend to keep up the illusion, and if I were you I should omit them (paying the Prophet all the same), and go slap dash into some such title as this—

"THE VISION OF NICHOLAS, IN SEVERAL FITS."
Not of course meaning to convey the idea that the old man is a-foaming at the mouth, but like the ancient ballads, which I dare say you may have heard of, Sir.

FIT THE FIRST.

Descend ye Mews!

I wouldst be inspired as quickly as possible, with a view to the Derby Double Number of the New Serious, so that I may be all there at what Lord Palmerston truly called " our Ishmael Games."

N.B. This is what they call an invocation, and is supposed to be wrote, not by NICHOLAS himself, but by another person, a young poet, as you will see as you go along.

Ha! the gentle influence descends, and a pleasurable sort of drowsiness seems pervading of my limbs, whilst my mental orbs acquire a range of vision to which Lord Rosse's telescope is blinkers.

THE SECOND FIT.

What do I see?

Ha! I see, reclining gently on a couch, the form of

an elderly man. His countenance beams with benevolence and genius. I wish he were my papa.

There can only be two old men who would look so innocent when they slept. It must be either Mr. PEABODY or MR. NICHOLAS. From the fact of there being sherry wine in the neighbourhood, I am inclined to think that it is more likely to be the latter than the former.

I will approach. His lips are moving. He breathes.

Although it is hardly a gentlemanly kind of thing to do, I will listen, and make my bets in accordance. He is a-talking in his sleep.

FIT III. (*to be printed with inverted kommers.*)

"Ah! deary me, deary me—and so they drove the horse-watchers off the ground, did they? Well, that's a good 'un, any how! Many's the time it was done to the old man himself, before I got respectable. How things do alter, to be sure!

"Hmnhh, grrh!" (Note—*This is* NICHOLAS *snoring.*)

"A poor old man, sir; but will do his best for his employers, bar none!

> " Methinks I see the famous Derby cracks
>   With jocund jockeys sitting on their backs,
>   Which first of all appears that sturdy scion
>   Of Stockwell and of Paradigm, Lord Lyon,
>   The betting being the Bank of England to a button
>   In favour of the property of MR. SUTTON!"

"Something queer about the feet—not Lord Lyon's—mine! If the Editor wants it done in poetry, he ought to pay double, at my time of life.

> " Raise, merry shepherds, raise the vocal shout :
>   The Lord may yet be beaten by the Lout ;

And if I had time I would write a long acrostic
On my original selection, Rustic."

"The rhyme ain't quite what it might be. Print it with a O.

"I envy not the invidious man
Who takes a liberty with bold Redan,
One of the finest as has ever ran!

"That's what they call a triplet, I believe!

"Fortune, fair maid, assist me! Prythee, stick, oh, lass,
To the good and gifted prophet, known as NICHOLAS!
Blue Riband next appears, with Bribery Colt,
The latter with a tendency to bolt;
And to make all serene on this occasion,
The Prophet's eagle eye selects Vespasian;
One more outsider might make all things pleasant,
Suppose, accordingly, the Knight o' the Crescent!
Whilst should another still upset the pot,
It may be found among Lord Glasgow's lot!"

"Pity they had to scratch Student, ain't it, Sir? He would have made the prettiest rhyme to prudent, with reference to place-betting, that a prophet could have wished.

"Hmnhh, grrh!" (Note.—*This is* NICHOLAS *snoring again.*)

FOURTH FIT.

"Subscribers, who sent you Gladiateur for Epsom and the Leger? Who sent you Ely for Ascot? Who has already enabled you to make a mint of money this present season?

"Stick to the old man, and he'll stick to *you!*

"As to Knurr and Spell, gentlemen, it shall all be done in good time; but as I am going to have it illustrated in mezzotint, you should hurry no man's cattle."

FIT FIVE.

A louder snore than ever resounded through the palatial apartment. For a moment the frame of NICHOLAS seemed convulsed with prophetic agonies. He muttered feebly, " Rustic—Redan—Blue Riband " . . . . .

And awoke.

———

There, sir, you have my idea of how to put it. You can please yourself about the punctuation, but mind that the authorgraphy is printed exactly as it is wrote.

And, in conclusion, Mr. Editor, and ye, my subscribers, the athletic men of merry, merry England, NICHOLAS will be upon the Downs himself, along with his relative, unless anything better should offer in the way of carriage accommodation and refreshment.

You may easily know the old man, gents; for he will wear a green veil, and have a race-glass slung behind me.

NICHOLAS.

———

NICHOLAS AT HIS ZENITH.

BELGRAVIA AGAIN.

Mr. Editor, my worthy friend, huzza! Let the welkin ring with jovial echoes! Let the joy-bells from a hundred steeples go clanging away, like—like mad! Let the beacon-fires be turned on immediate! And ye, thou sportive public, which was true and faithful to the Prophet whilst under a temporary cloud, fear not as I will desert thee now when NICHOLAS, speaking figurative, is a-lying down upon his back and basking in the effulgent radiancy of that glorious Orb of Day, known to men of science as the solar sphere.

His heart is in the right place, my good sir, and can feel for another. He have stood the bitter blasts of poverty, not to mention Mrs. Cripps, than whom perhaps a better old soul though a little not suited to NICHOLAS in his present fashionable orbit. He have likewise known what it is to eat the bread of dependence at the table of a vulgar, a purse-proud, and a stuck-up relative, and which I have often mentioned so, but will wash my hands off of him. Go to, ye pampered old skinflint!

Perhaps, my good young man, we had better put it all into little chapters, which make a countrybution look pictorial and variedsome. But, first of all, I say again, huzza!

CHAPTER ONE.—IN WHICH NICHOLAS EXPLAINS HIS PROPHECY.

It will be within the recollection of the Sportive Public that, at one period of his professional career, NICHOLAS was not particularly Barcelona nuts upon Lord Lyon. After my almost unprecedented success of Wednesday, I have no occasion to put a gloss upon the facts of the case, nor was the Prophet addicted to telling gross and wilful falsehoods when the truth seemed likely to answer as well. But whilst for some time he hesitated to say *positive* that the Lyon would be first, he kept on throwing out hints, which he hopes you may have acted on, my worthy editor, and ye my subscribers, as I did so myself. Turn, however, to your New Serious, page 94, and what do you find wrote down in poetry verses? And, dear sir, if you *had* any letters of gold, now would be your time to republish in that expensive but suitable medium,

NICHOLAS' PROPHECY OF THE ABSOLUTE WINNER!

> " Which, FIRST OF ALL, appears that sturdy scion
>   Of Stockwell and of Paradigm, LORD LYON!
>   *The betting being the Bank of England to a button,*
>   *In favour of the property of* MR. SUTTON ! "

There, do you call *that* a prophecy, or dost you not ?

So much for the first : and, sir, if you will just order one of your other contributors, than whom perhaps a better set of fellars for their station in life, though a little—well, well, never mind !—if, sir, you will tell him to look back to a previous number, it will there be triumphantly avouched that almost at the time when he was being driven nowhere in the betting, NICHOLAS sent you

THE BRIBERY COLT.

for a place.   As to the absolute third, the Prophet need scarcely remind his readers that he has all along, through good report and evil reporters, been constant in his asseverations that amongst the first three would be found

RUSTIC

And here, sir, the Prophet might be allowed to pause, and rest upon his laurels, speaking of course, meta-phorically, it being far too uncertain weather to go sleeping about in the open air.   To have named the first, second, and third in the great national, and I may even say hippical contest of the year would in itself be ample to satisfy what my friend Ben Disraeli—there's a states-man for you !—calls "a generous ambition."

But, sir, I did more !   *I did !*

And this, ye athletic men of merry, merry England, is the way in which I poetically commended to your notice *the absolute fourth* :—

> "One more outsider would make all things pleasant,
>   Suppose, accordingly, the KNIGHT OF THE CRESCENT!"

CHAPTER TWO.—IN WHICH NICHOLAS RETURNS TO HIS BELGRAVIAN HALLS.

My clear and definite prophecy—combined with the excellent pictorial hieroglyphic, where Lord Lyon is again shown as absolute winner and Rustic third, *vide* the cartoon, the artist however having scarcely done justice to my own leariness of expression, nor do I think such lies within the reach of any of our modern painters, bar none, naturally made me the cynosure of neighbouring eyes, and the splendid reception that was given to me and Mr. Sutton, sir, why ovations is a fool to it!

A good deal of natural curiosity was displayed as to the exact amount of the Prophet's winnings, especially by his relative. The answer made by NICHOLAS to that contemptible duffer, which has for months been trading, so to speak, upon my genius, and showing me about as his distinguished literary relative at sporting houses, though locking up the cellaret at home every night with the characteristic meanness of the lower orders of the commercial classes—the answer, sir, of the Prophet to that Thing, that purse-proud Vampire, though little enough to be proud of in that way *now*, NICHOLAS *having sold him with a wrong tip*—ha, ha, thou Baffled Tyrant! The answer of the old man was perhaps a little coarse, but it shut *him* up, anyways. It was, "You paddle yer own canoe, my bloke, and I'll paddle mine!"

5

Soon after which, the enormous success of NICHOLAS having been buzzed about, up came the landlord of my former mansion in Belgravia, which I left rather sudden you may remember, at the end of last year's racing season, and has not been let ever since, some people objecting to a previous tenant. It is not in the old man's heart to bear malice, and accordingly we made it up, over none of your cheap sherries, but a bottle of Sparkling Hock Wine, as soon as he had explained that in calling NICHOLAS "a confounded old swindler" he had not intended to cast the faintest slur either upon my commercial probity or my personal honour.

And, sir, as the song says, "Here we are again, here we are again, a jolly old dog am I!" You might give a feller a look up, sir, now and then. Such as befriended me in my adversity shall not be forsaken now I am again, so to speak, wallowing in the lapse of luxury and fashion!

NICHOLAS.

NICHOLAS "AT HOME AND ABROAD."

BELGRAVIA, *May* 31*st*, 1866.

MY DEAR EDITOR,—Previous to commencing of my countrybution for the present number, a word of explanation may be advisable with regard to my justly lamented absence from the last. You have no doubt received a number of letters, especially from the Upper Classes, amongst whom, I am proud to say, I am now one of them, complaining that NICHOLAS did not come up to time, and it may possibly have been suspected by the individuous that the old man was spoiled by success.

My dear young friend, never you believe no such a thing! You were true to him when Fortune darkly on me frowned, *vide* popular song, and he will be faithful and constant unto the New Serious until death do us part. The truth is, Sir, and ye, my subscribers, NICHOLAS have had a good deal—he does not mean to convey in the shape of liquor!—but he have had a good deal to distract his attention.

First and foremost, Sir, ever since the Prophet installed himself in his Belgravian mansion, he has been subjected to a course of systematic persecution by a Relative, which the old man will not soil his gloves by naming him more particular. That Connexion, Mr. Editor, that Bloodsucking Old Leech have been in the habit, not only of laying in wait for NICHOLAS at the corner of the Square, but of sending up his filthy old card at hours the most ill-convenient to a man of my habits, and asking for a few moments of conversation. The Prophet instructed his menials to say as he was not at home, but vain was such. Early one morning, for instance, the Extortionising Nuisance forced his way into the hall, and shouted up the staircase the following coarse remarks: "Now then, NICK, it ain't no go, you know! You ain't gone out yet, you know! Come down and meet a honest man, you double-faced old Leg!" To order him to be expelled from my mansion was the work of a moment—the twinkling of a bell-pull, so to speak; but NICHOLAS cannot shut his eyes to the fact that the use of such language must have produced a derogatorial and deucedly bad effect upon the minds of his domestic servants. Do you not think so yourself, Sir?

Accordingly, the Prophet determined to give him the slip, and run over to Paris to have a look at the International Race for the Grand Prix, pronounce Grong Pree.

Paris, Sir, the capital of France, and situated on the River Sane, may emphatically be denominated a metropolis, than whom I am sure a more amusing city, though perhaps a little immoral. The old man received what is generally termed an ovation.

I write my present countrybution on Wednesday morning, and in great haste, as you tell me you are obliged to go to Press early—which I think it is a great pity; but I am not going to shirk my duties as a Prophet, notwithstanding; and

MY ABSOLUTE WINNER OF THE CUP IS GLADIATEUR,
OF COURSE.

NICHOLAS.

P.S.—Whilst in Paris I made inquiries with regard to a favourite pastime, of which I am writing the History of it, but could not obtain any information worth speaking of.

NICHOLAS ON THE ARISTOCRACY AND HAMPTON RACES.

BELGRAVIA, *Wednesday*, 6 *June*, 1866.

MY DEAR EDITOR,—I have often told you in the columns of your New Serious, than which I am sure a more amusing print, though a little too cheap, especially when double-numbered, that after a storm comes a qualm. The exciting events of which the Turf have recently been the tappey, as the French say, are naturally succeeded by a period of comparative stagnation. What, sir, are the racing fixtures for the present week of grace? There is the Newton Meeting, and there is the

Windsor Meeting, and there is Hampton Races ; but all these, sir, are too insignificant to reward NICHOLAS for turning of his prophetic gaze towards them, like a peeler's bull's-eye. His reputation, which is now co-extensive throughout an empire, than which perhaps the sun never sits upon it, is based upon predictions relative to the really important hippic contests of the year, concerning which he will turn his back on nobody, bar none ! but leaves to the eleemosynary tipster and the casual tout the duty of describing inferior races.

Should any of your other countrybuters go to Hampton, let them beware of a seedy, middle-aged cove which is now going about the country a-bragging of his being my relative, and very likely trying to cadge a glass of sherry wine on the strength of it. That he is consanguineous NICHOLAS will not deny, nor that there may have been a period when the connexion was rather more advantageous to the Prophet than otherwise ; but, Mr. Editor, I have renounced him and I have shook him off. He is an extortionising duffer, and eats peas with his knife. There let him lay.

NICHOLAS.

P.S.—Shortly will be produced, illustrated by a series of encaustic tiles, my "History of Knurr and Spell."

The match between Oxford and Cambridge ended exactly as your prophet foresaw all day.

I know my faults as well as you or any man, but NICHOLAS in regard to that exciting contest may fearlessly lay claim to the merit of the strictest impartiality. You will probably be surprised to hear that the Prophet was not educated neither at Cambridge nor yet at

Oxford, though he have often been mistook for a University man by gents as was a little on, and if he had any offspring would certainly send him to the banks of the Cam or Isis, regardless of expense. The early culture of NICHOLAS was chiefly conducted of a Sunday, and the only thing as I can honestly say in its favour is that it was almost entirely of an eleemosynary character, through circumstances painful to recall. It was only in later years the Prophet really got fly to the Classics, than whom I am sure a more amusing author than Horatio Flaccus, though sometimes a little indelicate. Ah, well; *nunc vino pellite curas!* (Please see as this is put with the right authorgraphy, which I have copied it out with my own hand, and it means, as you may perhaps have heard, "Let us have a glass of sherry wine."

ANTICIPATIONS OF GOODWOOD.

BELGRAVIA, *July* 12, 1866.

MY DEAR YOUNG FRIEND,—One of those periods is now approaching which, despite my unrivalled success prophetically, I always regard them with a certain amount of nervousness and anxiety, having now a reputation to lose, not to mention lucre. The period, sir, is at hand when long before I know the result of the race I am called upon to name the winner; and it stands to reason, as I am sure my young friend will admit, who is the soul of honour, that such a course cannot have the moral certainty conferred by waiting until you know who has won and then giving of your tip in accordance. After all, however, why should the Prophet tremble? After the desert his banner even if for once he should prove unsuccessful.

Do not imagine, however, as NICHOLAS is in what may be called a blue funk. Gentlemen, I was never more sanguine of success in the whole of my vaticinatory career—no, not even when I sent ye the absolute first, second, and third for this year's Derby, nor prophesied the dead heat between General Peel and Ely in the Ascot of 1865.

GLORIOUS GOODWOOD !!!

Glorious Goodwood is exactly one of those meetings which NICHOLAS really enjoys. It may no longer be quite so select as it was in the days of my youth, before the railway brought down a lot of snobs from London into the intermediate neighbourhood; but it is still the resort of the Aristocratical, the Lavish, and the Gay. The noblemen of England, our best Palladiums, are emphatically all there. The Prophet will put up at Bognor, *unless invited to Goodwood itself by one who shall be nameless*, and always glad to see any of the more respectable of your readers; but I must draw the line somewhere, as I am sure my young friend will admit.

By the by, it is just possible that a Relative of mine, to whom I will only allude periphrastically by saying as he is very little better than an out-and-out old Thief, may skulk down to Brighton by the third-class excursion, and try to borrow money on the strength of a honoured name; but do not let him do so, subscribers, if ye ever want to see it again; and if he interferes with *me*, will have him locked up, and so I tell him, which well I know he sees your paper regular when able to afford it.

Now, then, Spirits of the Future, listen to the old

invocation, with which he invokes ye! Descend, ye Mews!

For the Goodwood Stakes, though seldom fond of giving ye the favourite, NICHOLAS feels bound to speak most favourably of

THE SPECIAL.

As for the Cup, the task of NICHOLAS is of a much easier description, and it is with a lively recollection of his former triumphs, which many is the bet I have won by him, that he sends ye

GLADIATEUR!

NICHOLAS.

NOT A HUNDRED MILES FROM SANDRINGHAM, NORFOLKSHIRE.

Wednesday, 18 *July*, 1866.

MY DEAR YOUNG FRIEND,—What I like about Albert Edward Princeps is that he bears no malice. You have already heard how he asked the Old Gentleman, who rode over him in Rotten Row to luncheon at Marlborough House, than where a better glass of sherry wine nor yet a more hearty welcome, and have seen a good deal of him ever since. Accordingly, when he asked your NICHOLAS, as one gentleman to another, whether he would like to run down to Norfolkshire, the Prophet immediately did so—not literally *running* down, the distance being far too great, not to mention the state of the temperature or my own period, but first-class express; and I warrant you, my dear young friend, the guards never tried to put *our* cigars out! We found all the aristocracy of the county assembled to receive us; and it was at once arranged that there should be a cricket-match between twelve of I Zingari and twelve of Norfolkshire. Mr. R. A. Fitzgerald, than whom a more amusing Irishman nor yet a fiercer slogger when the bowling gets a little loose, having incidentally mentioned that NICHOLAS was the real author of "Jerks in from Short Leg," the Prophet was immediately invited to occupy that honourable position in the cricket-field.

NICHOLAS, Sir, protested that at his period he could no longer dream of doing such; but was this his *real* motive?

No, my dear young friend, and ye, my subscribers, the athletic men of merry, merry England, *it was not!*

The Prophet, Sir and Gentlemen, knew that Another wanted to occupy that post, and although Another's modesty may have hindered him from saying so, yet it was not for NICHOLAS, especially after the accident, to cause any further ill-convenience to My Country's Hope.

Having arranged this delicate little affair quite amicable, NICHOLAS contented himself with scoring.

Our side, Sir, was extremely strong. Only one circumstance occurred to spoil the Old Man's thorough enjoyment of the day's play, and this was the fact that His Royal Highness was bowled out without making a single run. He is, however, far too good a sportive gentleman to be long down upon his luck, and added to which the ball was a really good one, and might not have been played successful by NICHOLAS himself.

To-morrow, Sir, let us hope as he will have better luck; and as for his hospitality can only say, without violating of the sanctity of private life, as it was sumptuous, nor have I ever put my prophetic legs under mahogany more thoroughly congenial.

This mark of consideration, Sir, will show you what is really thought of NICHOLAS by the highest in the land (*almost*), and will, I suppose, induce you to think no more of the anonymous slanders of the individuous and the mean.

The Old Man's Relative, I regret to say, came upon the ground in a state of the most low-lived intoxication, and laughed offensively when the wickets of Britannia's Hope was bowled; but, my dear young friend, forbearance *has* its limits, and the old worthless Tradesman had reached them at last. Sir, I sprung upon him like, though elderly, a tiger, and he is now out of harm's way in the custody of the Norfolkshire police, which I hope it may do him good.

Immersed in the whirlpool vortexes of aristocratical conviviality, and far more than Asiatical luxury, I have still a eye to my position as your trusted Sportive Editor, so will only repeat

GLADIATEUR FOR THE CUP.

NICHOLAS.

NICHOLAS IN THE HIGHLANDS.

GLENHOOLACHANACHAN.

MY DEAR YOUNG FRIEND, — In the Prophet's last communication, than which I am sure a more humorous production, it told you not to mind where he was, nor to trouble yourself about his address; but he do not now seek to mislead you, Sir, nor yet to keep you in the dark. He tells you frankly where he is, namely, in the land of brown Heath and shaggy Woods, who I suppose were both eminent natives of Caledonia, or else a baronet such as Sir Walter Scott was would not have so prominently alluded to them in his " Lay of the Last Marmion."

One of the reasons, my friend, why the old man do not mind giving you his address is that there is no regular post-office near the Glen, nor for miles and miles ; and as he took the precaution before leaving London to draw his salary for three weeks in advance, I do not so much mind your not writing to me until that period have expired. Donald will take this, on a pony, to the nearest village, the name of which, Sir, I have unfortunately forgotten of it, but it ends with a " h." Hoping you will not think the information vague, than whom perhaps.

  *   *   *   *   *

What I like about Highland sceneries is that after climbing about them, it is very nice to lie down on the flat of your Prophet's back, and have a weed and a nip, not meaning a tuft of heather and a near-wig, but a Havannah cigar and some whisky, the best of it being that in this climate you can take any quantity of it, Sir, with impunity—perfect impunity, which I have now been doing so! It sets one a-thinking, Sir, of a nobler age, when the old gentry of Caledonia (as it might be NICHOLAS) rose in arms at the head of their kilted clansmen for the young Chivy-Leah. The best of it being that in this quantity, Sir, you can take any climate with impunity.

  *   *   *   *   *

What you say, Evan, about my wearing of a kilt is ridicolas—perfectly ridicolas. There *was* a time :— well it have gone by, it have long gone by, Evan, and

at his present period, Sir, would be positively indecent,
by Jove! not to mention corpulence nor rheumatism.
Picturesque it may be, nor will NICHOLAS deny so; but
a proper dress for a man who is getting on in the whale
it is *not*, nor could ever have been so, and as for what
you say about George the Fourth, I despise such a
Hanoverian upstart, and would have fought you, or a
better man than you, Evan, a few years earlier, but I
am now too elderly. Though in perfect health, thanks
be, which I attribute to early hours, regular habits,
abundant exercise, and the quantity of impunity in this
climate—perfect impunity.

*   *   *   *   *

I am glad he have gone away. These Highland
Keepers, somehow, look down upon every one who is
not connected with the territorial aristocracy; and
although NICHOLAS have met the Duke of Sutherland
on a fire-engine, and the Duke of Hamilton on the
turf, yet the man evidently did not believe me when I
said so, and if you miss a solitary grouse, the old man's
shooting not being equal to what it was, he goes away
and laughs, and pretends it's one of the younger gillies,
he being enabled to do so—that's the best of it!—with
perfect impunity by the nature of the climate. Nor is
NICHOLAS at all sure, but what he *will* have another—
thank you, Evan, I am glad you have come back.

*   .   *   *   *   *

NICHOLAS.

P.S. 2.—How about a noble game? Have you received, Sir, the manuscript he sent you some time ago
containing his History of KNUER AND SPELL? If so, it
would have been only civil to say so.

MY DEAR YOUNG FRIEND,—Your letter have at length been forwarded to NICHOLAS by a special messenger, wherein you say as I have left you in the lurch, and call me an unprincipled old duffer, which is a form of speech that have been applied to me before, and I am sure you would not speak with such colloquial frankness not unless you meant it. Candour is one of your virtues, and so it is of mine, so the old man will not attempt to mislead you by any cock-and-bull story, as I do not think I could get you to believe, but tell you the honest truth, because it is tolerably sure to come out one way or another.

The fact is, then, my dear young Friend, that NICHOLAS have been again rioting in the lapse of luxury, and the Duke was so pleased with me that I found it quite impossible to get away from the Castle to my own shooting-box in this here Glen for the purpose of writing my copy. In fact, I have got rather into disgrace with one of my admirers, who shall be nameless beyond saying as he is Britannia's Hope and Cambria's Pride, by staying so long in the Highlands that I was unable to join him on the First of September in shooting of partridge birds; but H. R. H. have looked it over, Sir, he have looked it over, and is so good enough to say as the pleasure is merely postponed.

Everybody have been most kind, and even the keeper treats me less supercilious than what he used to do so. He was afraid as I should tell the Duke he had been impertinent, which I believe His Grace still retains the right of life and death over what are called his Downy-vassals, and could have hanged Evan up to a tree if there had been any in this part of Scotland, but, bless you, my dear fellow, there ain't so much as a gooseberry-bush.

The old man will now proceed to exercise his vaticinatory powers, and being now in the exact district where the famous "Second-Sight" is cultivated, will do so in the orthodox manner, he having been reading of Ossian and Sir Walter Scott.

THE ST. LEGER: A GAELIC FRAGMENT.

Dark are the torrents of Selma. The waters of Loch Awe are very deep. Misty, oh Morven, are thy mountains; and the foam-wreath of Corrievrechan is white as the sea-bird's wing.

Darker than the torrents of Selma is the winner of the Leger. The waters of Lock Awe are very deep; but NICHOLAS is deeper still. Mistier than the hills of Morven are the enigmatical prophecies of your individuous contemporaries; and whiter than the sea-bird's wing, whiter than the foam-wreaths of Corrievrechan are the hairs upon the head of the old man, than whom perhaps.

Behold him on the mountain-top, or thereabouts. On his prophetic countenance Genius and Benevolence are struggling for pre-eminence. The fight is a draw.

He reverses his plaid, and draws it round him, shrouding his noble head (though he *have* been called "an unprincipled old duffer" where least expected) in its mystical folds. His form goes into epileptical convulsions, and he reels to and fro as if he had had too much to drink. Perhaps he *have*.

[Never you believe it, my dear young Friend! Not *you!*]

Howls the wind. Scream the tall pines in horrible

unison. Shout ye remarkable old cataracts! Hark, my subscribers, to the wild words of the Second-Sighter:—

"The Absolute Winner of the St. Leger it will be Lord Lyon, and no flies!

On Knight of the Crescent and on Savernake you may equally keep your eyes!

For the Prophet have never deceived a man, and he never was known to *trick* a lass.

So gents, put your money, and ladies, your gloves on the final selection of   NICHOLAS."

P.S. 2.—Instead of calling me "an unprincipled old duffer," it would be more courteous to tell me what you have done with the MS. of my "Knurr and Spell."

———

UNPARALLELED TRIUMPH OF THE PROPHET! NICHOLAS ENTIRELY RIGHT AGAIN!! WHAT A MAN HE IS, TO BE SURE!!!

BELGRAVIA.

MY DEAR YOUNG FRIEND,—NICHOLAS have now returned from his long vocation among the Highland hills in Scotlandshire, where his heart still is, a-chasing the wild deer and hunting the roe, so to speak, not as I ever did so, it being far too violent for my period, and preferred having a crack at a grouse bird from the top of a pony or else lying down on your back and admiring of the sceneries.

All as it is now necessary for the Prophet to say about Caledonia is as no better whisky can be found throughout the United Kingdom of Great Britain, than whom perhaps on which the sun himself never sets; but the longest holiday it must come to a end, my dear young feller, and I travelled right through to London.

On arriving in a city which it have been wittily described as the modern Babylon, NICHOLAS found as the whole town was ringing with his name. The prophecy which he vaticinated of in your last impression was the theme of universal everybody's talking of it.

You are so extremely fond, young man, of calling the grey-headed and the good a "unprincipled old duffer," that it may well be asked you whether, even supposing me to be "old" and "unprincipled," NICHOLAS is so much of a "duffer" after all?

What were the three horses given by him for the St. Leger in your last impression?

Messrs. Printers & Co., please put it tabular.

SELECTIONS OF NICHOLAS.	ACTUAL RESULTS.
Lord Lyon.	Lord Lyon.
Savernake.	Savernake.
Knight of the Crescent.	Knight of the Crescent.

This fact, sir, speaks for itself.

I do not think as I shall ever write for you again. The emolument ain't much to speak of, not to a man as has made pots of money by own unaided genius, and I do *not* like being called "an unprincipled old duffer" every week. Who would?

At any rate, perhaps you may think it worth your while to comply with the terms of the Prophet's Ultimatorium; which I annex, and hope as all may yet be well, for I hate quarrelling with a friend when there is scarcely anything to be got by it.

My Ultimatorium.

1. You must rise my salary.

2. You must withdraw the expression "unprincipled old duffer."

3. You must print my copy exact as I send it, and no humbugging about authography or pointuation.

4. You must always speak of me more respectful, both in public and private.

5. We will have a little dinner at a place I know.

6. Sherry wine.

7. No more gammon about Knurr and Spell. Fork out the Manuscript, my boy!

NICHOLAS.

EDITORIAL NOTE.—We accept this Ultimatorium, so far as we are able. The St. Leger Prophecy was certainly admirable, but we have *not* received the Manuscript of Knurr and Spell.

MY DEAR YOUNG FRIEND,—NICHOLAS have his faults, but rancorous maliciousness and bearing a grudge is not one of them. You have done the handsome thing by your Prophet; you have retracted expressions which had a tendency to vex him, such as "unprincipled old duffer;" and I must say as you show every desire to be again on friendly terms with one whose genius has helped to make the paper what it is, *ergo*, second to none, bar none, as A Sportive Organ and A Racing Guide.

In accordance, the clouds of animosity and my feeling really annoyed by such low language have rolled away like the mists of the mountain from the crags of

Glenhoolachanachan, Scotlandshire, where I was, you know. I accept your retractation and my own rise of salary ; and I will prophesy for you honest and true whenever I see my way to a real good thing.

The future Historian, Sir, when speaking of my St. Leger's Prophecy of 1866 shall never have it in his power to say as NICHOLAS was a corruptor of youth, nor yet as I wilfully led them into Sweeps. I may, or I may not, be what some of my friends are good enough to call me so,

NICHOLAS, THE PRINCE OF PROPHETS.

I may, or I may not, have given you first, second, and third in that noble race which is named above ; I may, or I may not, be rather more up to a thing or two than absolutely a "doddering old fool," as one of your anonymous correspondents calls me, or an " un-principled old duffer," as you used to call me so your-self, deny it if you can, or "a pampered and purse-proud Ingrate," as I am often termed by a Relative to whom I am sure no one was ever more kind to him ; at any rate, the character and career of NICHOLAS can safely be allowed to speak for themselves. And, my dear young Friend, if by any chance, you know—it *might* happen ; we can never tell!—if it *should* occur that any of your correspondents should think it only the right sort of thing to offer him a Public Testimonial, for I know as it have been mooted in certain influential circles, all I have to say is that though I may not posi-tively want it, nor do I, and would scorn to cadge for it, yet if your subscribers should come forward with their fivers or even their humble quids, it would be false pride in me to decline such a Memorial. But, of course, I do not care about a Statute, nor have I ever done so.

What you say, Sir, about not having received the MS. of my " Knurr and Spell," it is indeed a heavy blow to lose the literary labour of years. Do you not think as I might bring an action against the Post-office? It was a noble work, though I say it; but, per-haps, Sir, it have since turned up?

NICHOLAS.

PROPOSED TESTIMONIAL.

We have received the following communication :—

To the Editor of Fun.

LONDON.

MR. EDITOR,—Do you not think, Sir, that the time have now arrived when some public recognition ought to be made of the genius, perseverance, and integrity displayed by your Sportive Prophet? Sir, MR. NICHOLAS is not personally known to me, though I have often wished as I had the honour of his acquaintance, in consequence of which this proposal is made entirely upon public grounds, nor do I wish to obtrude myself.

Week after week, Sir, your organ, than whom I am sure a more amusing periodical, though I wonder how you do it for the money—week after week, Sir, your organ have been enriched, not to say immortalised, by the countrybutions of that illustrious man, and seldom, indeed, is it but what his tips have proved that right you are. I have myself, Sir, long been in the habit of backing the selections of MR. NICHOLAS, whereby I have realized a handsome sum of money, and so may any one who will follow him faithful, and it is therefore

from feelings of pecuniary gratitude united to those of
epistolary admiration that I suggest the least thing as
can fairly be done for him is a Testimonial.

Sir, if you will survey the historic scroll of your
New Serious, you will find that the Prophet have almost
invariably been all there, or thereabouts; selecting with
a unerring eye the future winner of the hippic and
equestrian jousts, and often sending of him when he is
at outside prices, thereby enabling you to put the pot on
heavy. It might be tedious, Mr. Editor, to recapitulate
all the achievements of your good and gifted " old man,"
as he playfully calls himself in your organ, though I
daresay not a bit older after all than many as pretends
to look down on him.   What have he not foretold, sir?
His accuracy it have become poorverbial, and I am quite
snre that every right-minded betting-man in Great
Britian's glowing Hemisphere must look upon him as
a True British Prophet, and a Benefactor to his Fellow
Man !

As such, Sir, MR. NICHOLAS deserves a public Recognition and Memorial; and it only needs a few well-
known names for to set it agoing, and no flies. ADMIRAL
ROUS would perhaps not object to be one of the com-
mittee, and I believe that though he once ordered
NICHOLAS off Newmarket Heath, such was done before
the Prophet had attained celebrity.   Many of Britannia's
Aristocracy, to whom the old man is well beknown,
would of course join in, and I do not think it altogether
impossible but what H. R. H. might be induced to come
forward and rally round a brother sportsman, than
whom he well know NICHOLAS to be so.

Sir, the time have gone by when Statutes were all
the go ; nor from what I have heard tell of the Prophet's

physical appearance, though pleasing and genial, do I think as he would look well in a Statute, either equestrian or not so, but otherwise. Besides, statutes after all, are incentuals to vanity and graven images. No, Mr. Editor! Let us give *practical* proof of our regard for NICHOLAS. Do not let us waste the money in brass or marble :—*let us give it to him in hard cash ;* and no one will be more happy to contribute his mite than

AN OLD AND RESPECTABLE SUBSCRIBER.

P.S.—We might also give him a few dozen of Sherry wine.

[EDITORIAL NOTE.—NICHOLAS, this trick is unworthy of you! The handwriting is disguised, but we know your style of composition, you artful old man!]

BELGRAVIA.

MY DEAR YOUNG FRIEND,—I don't think I have ever enjoyed a heartier laugh than what it gave me in the last number of your New Serious, under the head of "Proposed Testimonial," where you have a kind of a lark with the old man, such as saying in an Editorial footnote, "NICHOLAS, this trick is unworthy of you." Capital, my dear young Friend, capital! It is just those kind of light, sparkling, genialistic remarks which endear you not alone to the old man, though I was always very fond of you from the time you asked me to contribute, nor have it diminished since you rose my salary, but also to the athletic men of merry, merry England. Why, of course, my dear young Friend, it was all a joke! I never thought as I could take *you* in, nor am I quite sure as I would do so if I could ; but I thought the notion might amuse you, and I felt sure your perspicacity would put the general reader on his guard, than whom I don't think much of him as a rule, he being easily gammoned by literary men. I am accordingly delighted to observe as you have taken it in the proper spirit, such as it was meant to be; and this friendly little interchange of good-natured banter will, I am sure, only increase our feelings of mutual endearingment and reciprocation.

At the same time, the Prophet owes it to himself—and debts of that particular description are exactly the last as he would ever forget to pay!—to declare that he really sees nothing at all ridiculous in the proposal of a Testimonial standing on its own merits.

Under these circumstances, please be good enough to acknowledge

SUBSCRIPTIONS FOR THE NICHOLAS TESTIMONIAL.

Votary of the Chase	...	...	£1	0	0
A Sportive Bung	...	...	1	0	0
			2	0	0

Every little helps; and Rome, as your classical scholarship and knowledge of architecture will remind you, was not built in a day.

NICHOLAS.

P.S. 2.—We had better offer a reward—at least, *you* had—for the recovery of my History of Knurr and Spell. It is the only work on the subject ever written in the English language; nor do I think the game was even known to the ancients.

MY DEAR YOUNG FRIEND,—The weather having at
length taken a change, and high time it did so, during
the present autumnal equinox, NICHOLAS determined to
have another spell of what his friends the barristers call
the Long Vocation. The vocation of the Prophet is
always as long as ever he can make it ; for although I
am fond of London, and of those gilded *salons* where the
élite of the *beau monde* display their *éclat* in the most
researchey manner, yet the old man is likewise partial to
what Milton, than whom I am sure a more lofty-minded
bard, though, as to reading *Paradise Lost* right through,
it's all nonsense, and it can't be done, was accustomed
to describe as "fresh fields and pastors new." Accordingly, when a young Friend of mine—and mind you
put "Friend" with a big F, or he mightn't like it—
asked me to come down and have a crack at the phea-
sant birds, the old man instantaneously replied " Done
with you, Sir !" and is again rioting in those lapse of
luxury so frequently mentioned in your columns.

The offer of my Relative to be your Sportive Editor
for half the salary at present paid to NICHOLAS is exactly
what I should have expected from his low-minded disposition, he having been always notorious in our family
as a mean old hunks, and I told him so myself the
moment I was fortunate enough to escape from his
filthy clutches (metaphorical), but where it says, " I
taught him everything he knows, and have often fed
him on the fat of the land at a time when he hadn't a
decent coat to his back," why, Sir, it is all mendacity ;
for if *he* calls boiled beef and carrots "the fat of the
land," *I* don't ; and as to not having a decent coat,
why, I never pretend to be a dressy man, nor rigged

myself out with mother-of-pearl buttons, like a conceited old publican; and as to his teaching me all I know, why all the more credit to me for picking of it up so quick, and bringing my pigs to a better market than what *he* could, the vanity-glorious old duffer! I am glad to hear as you declined his offer; but I hope he will not insist upon a personal interview and explaining all the circumstances, as you would find him a most disagreeable companion, he always smelling badly of rum and water whenever able to afford such.

The other letters, or most of them, are much more satisfactory; and I am sure you will be glad to hear that the movement for a testimonial, which you so kindly set on foot, is rapidly advancing with gigantic strides towards a pinnacle of success, than which I am sure none more deserving of a complete ovation. Some of the foremost men in the land, though I have not the honour to be personally known to all of them, have rallied round the old Prophet, as you will perceive, Sir, from the following list of contributions to

THE NICHOLAS TESTIMONIAL.

	£	s.	d.
Amount already acknowledged ...	£2	0	0
Dean Close (so it says)	1	1	0
The Earl of Shaftesbury (I think)...	0	0	3
A Student of the Prophecies ...	0	5	4
A Millionaire's Mite	0	0	2
A Working Man	5	0	0
One who hates oppression	0	1	0
Collected by the Scottish National Nicholas Committee (2,137 sub-scribers)	0	10	4½
"Sportmans" (Paris)	0	0	9

An Admirer of Talent	...	...	0	2	6
Gentlemen employed at Mr. Miff's the eminent butcher's	...	...	1	2	6
A Poor Curate	...	...	...	5	0	0
Liberality (a penny short—stamps)			0	0	11

£15 4 9½

NICHOLAS.

P.S. 2.—Why do you not answer my repeated inquiries with regard to my Knurr and Spell? *What have you done with it?*

NICHOLAS ON THE CAMBRIDGESHIRE.

BELGRAVIA, 18th October, 1866.

MY DEAR YOUNG FRIEND,—You will perceive from my superscription as I have at length returned to town, than which I am sure a chillier, nor yet a muggier metropolis, though a little gay. The Prophet is as fond of London as any man, bar none; but when you have rheumatism in your left shoulder, not to speak of a racking cough which keeps him awake half the night, it is only natural for to grumble at the climate, and wish as I was in the sunny south, where the warmth is.

However, the voice of Duty is one to which the Prophet is never indifferent, and accordingly tore myself from the dear fellows down in Norfolkshire, who wept bitterly when NICHOLAS drove away, and hurried back to my town residence—in itself a monument to the genius of one who raised himself from a comparative lowly position, though always respectable, to my present pinnacle. But, as to the *pleasure* of coming back, my dear young Friend, don't you believe in such! Why, the bills as have been accumulating—but suppose we change the subject, with merely the remark that now or never is the day, and now or never is the hour, to come forward with the Testimonial.

The last of the Great Turf Events of 1866 is now at hand, namely, to wit, the Cambridgeshire at the Newmarket Houghton Meeting, and so here, my friends and patrons, the Athletic Men of merry, merry England, is my

PROPHECY FOR THE CAMBRIDGESHIRE.

LOOK OUT FOR PROSERPINE, ACTÆA, AND SCARBOROUGH.

And now, Sir, with regard to another subject of (I may say) even more world-wide importance, please be good enough to acknowledge the following

SUBSCRIPTIONS TO THE NICHOLAS TESTIMONIAL.

Amount already acknowledged ...	£15	4	9½
One who has won thousands through following MR. NICHOLAS	0	1	0
	£15	5	9½

This can hardly be considered a good week for the Movement, Sir; but I daresay as we shall soon have a rally round. Do you not think another of your nice little Editorial Paragraphs might help to make the public a little less backward in coming forward?

NICHOLAS.

P.S.—If you don't give me *some* explanation about my Knurr and Spell, I shall be reluctantly obliged to take legal proceedings against your publisher.

BELGRAVIA.

My DEAR YOUNG FRIEND,—The racing season is over! At a former period of my career such intelligence would have blighted my young hopes, and plunged me into an impecunious ocean of casual postage-stamps, picked up from the innocent, the childish, the linendrapery, and the good. Formerly the end of festivity upon the British Turf was likewise, with NICHOLAS, the end of having anything to eat, excepting what might be attained promiscuously from private charity, such as a bullock's heart or tripe, than which I am sure anything more nourishing, though a little low.

Thanks to my own industry and acuteness, NICHOLAS have now attained a pinnacle from which he is not merely sure of his daily bread, but, if I liked to do so, might cover it with treacle as thick as a paving-stone. The worst of it is, my dear young Friend, that indigestion have marked me for her own. In the hours of penury my appetite was excellent; whilst now the Prophet feels quite squeamish after breakfast, though he may only have had a few eggs, some ham, rolls, a chop or two, kidneys and a little marmalade spread out upon toast, and etcetera.

Before, Mr. Editor, we treat the racing season of 1866 as entirely a thing of the past, you will perchance allow me the privilege of a brief interrogatory explanation.

Subscribers all, during the mad and confused intermingling of prophetical opinions naming of at least a dozen horses, was there any one who restricted his selection for the Cambridgeshire to Three?

Subscribers.—Yes, there was! One—*only* one! Methinks 'twas gentle NICHOLAS.

Gentle Nicholas.—Oh, you only think so, dost ye?

Subscribers.—Now, look here, old man. We are very well aware as it was thou. Let us unite our voices. What did the Prophet prophesy?

Subscribers.
Gentle Nicholas. } (*uniting their voices.*)—Actæa.

Posterity.—And so I found it on referring to the Number.

❋   ❋   ❋   ❋   ❋   ❋

A truce to poesy. Let us return to the non-avoidabilities of daily life.

Sir, I am a Conservative; I have been so ever since I was able to look down upon my fellow-man from a pinnacle of pecuniary superiority. But, my dear young Friend, with reference to the manuscript of my "History of Knurr and Spell," do you not think, Sir, as it is quite possible the new Postmaster-General and his staff may have been just a little on the loose? that, in point of fact, they may have rather mislaid the manuscript in general than delivered it at your office in particular? My position is one of no ordinary difficulty nor yet embarrassment. The History involves the research and the miscellaneous reading of a lifetime, from penny papers up to getting a ticket for the British Museum; there are references and quotations in that book for which the originals have very probably been cut up and destroyed; and here am I, Sir, a sort of sportive Buckle or an athletic Grote, as will possibly go down to his grave, "unwept, unhonoured, and unstrung!" Be it so; only I warn you again as I will bring an action against the Proprietor.

One word, Sir, on a topic in which you have kindly taken the utmost interest. Bless you, my dear young

Friend, and be good enough to print (the publisher said it ought to be put as an advertisement and paid for, but never you mind *him!*) the following list of subscribers to

THE NICHOLAS TESTIMONIAL.

Amount already acknowledged...		£15	5	9½
THE O'DONOGHUE	...	...	1	0	0
MR. POPE HENNESSEY	...	...	1	0	0
The People of Ireland	...	...	2	0	0
The Irish People	...	...	2	0	0
Rara Avis (*bless her!*)	...	...	0	0	2
		£21	5	11½

NICHOLAS.

P.S. 2.—Nothing more.

ANTICIPATIONS OF COMPIEGNE.

BELGRAVIA.

MON CHER AMI,—Whatever may be your Prophet's failings it can scarcely be denied as NICHOLAS sent you his copy last week regular. And, oh, my dear young Friend, you have no idea what a comfort it was for the old man to get back! I don't say a word against the Navskoi Perspective; nor yet a syllable against Alexander II., than whom I am sure I was never treated more hospitable, though a little pompous; but NICHOLAS have now arrived at a period of life when it is a great deal more agreeable for to sit down and drink gin-and-water at your own fireside than what it is for to wallow in barbaric splendour, and then have half your toes froze off in a droschky. When the Prophet was young, he often used for to have a lark with snowballing along the

streets where he was then being brought up; and many
is the respectable elderly tradesman than whom NICHOLAS
have given him one for his nob. Ha, ha, ye elderly
tradesman!

It will, I think, be admitted that a Friend of mine
behaved every inch like a Prince of Wales; and that
We won golden opinions, as Shakespeare says, from all
kinds of coves.

When I came home, Sir, I was a-thinking of just
writing you a Review of the Racing Season of 1866;
and no earthly power should have prevented the old
man from doing so had he not suddenly received an
invitation to what NICHOLAS will take the liberty of calling a Friendly Shore.

There don't breathe a man, my dear young Friend,
whom is more attached to Britannia the pride of the
ocean, the home of the brave and the free, the shrine of
each patriot's devotion, chorus, hurrah for the red, white,
and blue! These have been my principles from early
youth. I would rather have boiled beef and carrots beneath the meteor-flag of England which shall yet terrific
burn, 'til danger's troubled night be o'er and the star of
peace return, chorus, and the Morning Star return,
than what I would sit down to a luxurious dinner *alley
Roose*, which half the kickshaws made him ill, and was
over-persuaded for to taste an olive, than whom anything more likely for to disagree with men previously
unaccustomed, especially it being a fine fat Spanish one,
and no flies.

It is, however, pretty generally understood amongst
what is called the *élite* of the *beau monde* that a royal—
much more, an Imperial—invitation is equivalential to a
command. What the old man really wanted, Sir, was

rest—a sort of quiet vocation during which he might show himself about London, especially at many a Sportive House whose Bungs used to look down upon him contumelious, and prove to such as he had not come home empty-handed from the City of the Czar. N.B.—Some people call it " City of the Tsar; " but such spoils the alliteration, besides looking like a sneeze.

Rest, however, and your old man have long been strangers, and it is one of the penalties of popularity that you are not master of your own time. As a private individual, Nicholas only wants his glass of sherry wine and a friendly gossip along of an old acquaintance over *Bell's Life;* but if—mind, I say *if*—if a Neighbouring Sovereign—or, perhaps, to put it more accurate, a Neighbouring Napoleon—sends over a special currier to ask you to come and hob-nob with him at Compayne, why the Prophet would be downright rude if he was to say, "No, your Majesty : not so ; I prefer my own fireside."

I will endeavour to keep you posted up with regard to our revels, though Nicholas is not the sort of old man to violate the sanctitudes of private life ; and I daresay as I may have a look-in at a stable or two afore I come home.

Meanwhile, I have only one bit of advice, which please tell the printers to print it like a tip—

KEEP THE TESTIMONIAL A-GOING.

NICHOLAS.

P.S. 2.—If you have found the MS. of my " History of Knurr and Spell," please have it done into French, and send it over. I think a certain party might like to see it.

P.S. 3.—Prepaid !

"Who would have thought the Old Man had so much blood in him."—*Shakespeare.*

A LA COMPAYNE.

MONSIEUR LE REDACTEUR,—Without violating the sanctitudes, I may safely tell you that we are all as happy as the days are long—not that the days *are* long just now, such being against the almanack, and talking of almanacks I have bought several French ones and brought them down along with me, with the view to picking up the colloquial tone usual in high society amidst our Lively Neighbour; and so he may be, but the claret wine as he gives me do not agree with the Prophet's inside.

I cannot say that the French Court quite comes up to my notions of dignity. It is not for NICHOLAS to shy a lot of mud at the other members of the Fourth Serious; but you will hardly believe it, Sir, such are the influences of Levelism and Democracy that authors, my dear young Friend, *authors* are positively received at Court ! ! ! Oh, England—oh, my home ! Oh, Land of Freedom, when did a mere literary chap pollute Windsor Castle ? Not if the Genius of Britannia knows it. It may be objected that NICHOLAS is himself a man of letters ; but remember as that is not his only profession. NICHOLAS is also a betting-man ; and I quite agree with the *Saturday Review* —than whom a more truly aristocratic organ, though a little not-quite-so-good-as-it-used-to-be—that Literature is only respectable when combined with other avocations, such as not being employed at the bar.

However, the Prophet fell in with the prevalent tone of the place. I visited his Majesty simply on my footing as a English gentleman well known at Newmarket; but I am not ashamed of my contributions to your periodical press; and, accordingly, when I saw that Lewis Napoleon was fond of literature, I did what I could to amuse him. We held a little council, some of us literary men. There was me and Edmond About—pronounce it like Abboo, as though an African Chief—and we thought we would draw up just a little kind of seasonable trifle for him. It have not yet come out; but I send you the rough draft of your Prophet's contribution. I have tried to make it instructive as well as amusing—

ODE.

To the Imperial Prince's Highness, Etc., etc., etc.

All hail, ye young, but yet imperial cove!
    Your father is a celebrated man;
He may be led, perhaps, but won't be drove,
    And such was Nicholas when life began!

Like Nicholas, *he* had his ups and downs;
    But now they both are taking of their ease:
Me in Belgravia, fingering the browns!
    Him ruling Europe, from the Toolerees!

We both of us despise the vulgar crowd;
    We both of us respect the Prince of Wales;
One of his palaces is called Saint Cloud,
    Another's appellation is Versailles.

Hail, then, ye child of empire adolescent!
    Hail, then, ye beaming, bright, and beauteous Scion!
And may your father always keep things pleasant
    With Nicholas's Home, the British Lion!!

NICHOLAS.

P.S.—I am teaching the Imperial Prince how to play at Knurr and Spell. I think he will be very fond of it, bless his little heart, by and by; but at present it is a link too many for him.

NICHOLAS ON CHRISTMAS.

"That old man eloquent."—JOHN MILTON. Sonnet to the
Lady Margaret Ley.

BELGRAVIA.

MON CHER JEUNE AMI,—It is all very well to be a
man of fashion, but every true-born Briton ought to
remember as it is his first duty to be patriotic. While
at Compayne the most flattering offers were made to
the Prophet; and I *have* heard that it was in contem-
plation in *certain quarters* to give him a place tempo-
rarily vacated by Colonel Fleury, only at a higher salary,
my tastes being, perhaps, more lavish.

I am back in London; I trust it may not appear
bumptious if I say I am back in Belgravia. I am back,
after a serious of foreign travel, which expands the
mind; and you may actually expect to behold some of
the results in your pages. My mind, however, has its
peculiarities; and one of such is that it will not be able
to expand unless you raise my wages. I put it to you,
mon cher jeune ami, or—as we say in St. Petersburg—
chrescovitch nejeff wrakoski—as I am well worth my
salt; and really, at this sweet, and holly, and festive
time of year, the bills are coming in after a fashion—
especially my tailor's bill, which his clothes were long
after *any* fashion !—truly dreadful to behold; but even
worse for to pay them.

Besides, I have now a position to maintain; whilst
at one time I had nothing to maintain but myself, and
could do so on the cheap ! You may remember, sir, that
last Christmas I was the Pio Nino of my period. I was
abandoned to the mercy of the world; and I am bound
to say as such never came near me. I was thrown
(putting it metaphorical) into the lap of Mrs. Cripps's

lodgings at Bermondsey, than whom though a more
respectable person, yet if you happened to be a day behind with your rent, her language, Sir, was equal to
ALLOCUTIONS! Even then, sir, what NICHOLAS will call
the instinct of hospitality survived the possession of
capital; and I asked all your staff to come and dine
with me. How many came? *One* came. It was Moosoo
Jean Goodin, which always told me he was banished
from France because a Republican, though I *have* heard
at Compayne, that it was more in the nature of em-
bezzling funds. The rest of your contributors held
aloof—they knew I had only a bit of beef to offer, and
they turned up their noses at it, not as it was at all
necessary for them to do so, Nature in many cases,
though I name no names, having done so already; and
I was left alone until protected by a Relative whose
kindness to me at that period has long been cancelled
by the most low-lived serious of persecutions.

I have no doubt as you will rise my wages; but I
cannot expect you to do so until the beginning of the
new year, and as my travelling expenses have been
heavy, I shall not repeat the blunder of Christmas 1865.
I am in a position to enjoy a luxurious meal; I hope
your other contributors are the same; but

NICHOLAS WILL DINE ALONE ON CHRISTMAS DAY!

NICHOLAS.

P.S. Ah! what a festive season it is! and don't
it seem to open the heart, like?

P.S. (2). Now is the very time, my dear young
Friend, for you to bring out my "History of Knurr and
Spell." The public interest in the subject will pass
away, if you don't look precious sharp.

NICHOLAS ON THE TENDER PASSION AND THE CHESTER CUP.

"An Old Man, my lord, an Old, Old Man!"
DICKENS. *Oliver Twist*. Fagin.

BELGRAVIA.

MY DEAR YOUNG FRIEND,—I need scarcely remind *you*, at your period in Life's morning march when the spirits are young, that we are now close upon St. Valentine's Day, than which a more affectionate annual-versary though a little gay. *My* time for sending of poetical compositions through the medium of the penny post, addressed to my Heart's Delight, have long, long since departed; and, in point of fact, NICHOLAS never took very kindly to such a practice, which it involves a preliminary expenditure to which his resources were not invariably adequate. And where is the use of such after all, my dear young Friend, they being anonymous and not signed with your name?

If the Object of your Affections is pretty, she is sure to get plenty of valentines let alone yours, for there's more fools in the world than one; and you may after-wards find an opportunity of hinting as you sent the most expensive. If she is *not* pretty, she will be glad enough to get courted at all, Sir, without looking out for extravagant missives. This may appear a little mean, my dear young Friend, but you may be quite sure as it is true philosophy and human nature.

I *have* loved, no doubt; and in early youth there was a Being which had been left a ham and beef shop by her First, in Lambeth, behind the counter of which I might have made a pretty penny, and she had, also, something put by; but she could never abide the Prophet after he had got her to put a half-sovereign into a Derby sweep which she did not happen to draw the winner; or, rather, NICHOLAS did not happen to draw it for her, and she could never be got to believe but what he had embezzled the money and spent it in liquor, as perhaps he had.

My young Friend may also remember that in the latter part of 1865, when NICHOLAS was temporally under a cloud, and residing in lodgings down at Bermondsey, there were certain little love-passages, so to speak, along of me and Mrs.—there, I almost forget the good woman's name—Mrs.—Mrs.—yes, Cripps! and a very well-meaning person she was for her station in life and previous bringing-up. The Prophet will hardly deny but what he *may* have given her occasionally a friendly squeeze, nor yet that she *may* have exclaimed, "For shame, Mr. NICHOLAS; go away, do, you naughty aggerawaiting old wagabone!"—(for, Sir, she was both illiterative and plain-spoken)—but these facts only prove my happy disposition and knack of accommodating myself to circumstances. As for anything like a formal promise of marriage, the idea is ridicolas; and if ever I entertained such, it was at once dismissed when I was kindly took up by a relative, whose subsequent disgraceful conduct to me would draw tears from a Board of Guardians.

I do not say that I shall never marry; but, if I do, it will not be from any foolish and romantic notions, but with a view to increasing the stability of my finances, and to improving of my social position, which, after all, is unpleasantly precarious when so much depends upon your judgment of a horse, and the Turf getting wickeder every day of its existence.

Nevertheless, here is a bumper-toast, gentlemen, to

all true lovers; and may they meet with a great deal more happiness in matrimonial life than it is the Old Man's candid opinion they are at all likely to enjoy!

Now then for the Chester Cup, though, of course, this must be looked upon as a very long shot considering the period. *You* may do as you like, gentlemen; but if you do as the Prophet does, you will make haste to put some money on the game little Lecturer, whilst keeping safe with Rama. There, gents: *other* tipsters are giving you *twenty horses* against the field! Stick to NICHOLAS!! *Vivat Nicholas!!!*

NICHOLAS!!!!

P.S. (2.)—If you do not precious soon find my MS. about "Knurr and Spell" you and me may have words.

P.S. (3.)—You may have observed that my recent countrybutions have been preceded by a quotation as a motto. I have engaged a gentleman connected with the press to look them out for me at a shilling per motto and his wine. *I* think this ought to be paid by the Proprietor of *Fun*. What do *you* think?

PERSONAL EXPLANATIONS.—INTERESTING CORRESPONDENCE.

> "And thus I prophesy that many a Thousand . . . .
> And many an Old Man's sigh!"
> > *Shakespeare.* Henry VI., Third Part, Fifth Act, Sixth Scene.

> " Lord, Lord, how subject we Old Men are to this vice of lying!"
> > *Shakespeare.* Henry IV., Second Part, Third Act, Second Scene.

BELGRAVIA.

MY DEAR YOUNG FRIEND,—I do not think it would do you a bit of harm if you were a little more civil to some of your contributors, than whom perhaps I am myself one of the oldest and certainly one of the most respectable. I have just received a note from you which, if it is intended by way of a joke, why, where no offence is meant, none such is taken, and can stand a laugh at my own expense—which I also have to stand a good many other things at my own expense!—as well as any Prophet within Britannia's isle, bar none; but if it is meant serious, you should have thought twice before addressing NICHOLAS in a manner calculated to bring his grey hairs to the bottle, and drive me to despair. The time *may* come, Sir, when you will not be able to read the following lines (coarse and offensive *I* call 'em!) without a pang, nor yet without a pair of spectacles, for you yourself may yet become an Old Man, and be chaffed by the young and gay.

"FUN OFFICE.

"DEAR NICHOLAS,

"1. For the last two weeks you have omitted to send in your copy.

"2. For the last two weeks you have not omitted to send for your salary.

"3. Did you ever hear of a sporting character called Swindells?

"4. Does it ever occur to you that you deserve to be locked up?

"5. I have just received a proposal from an intelligent young man.

"6. He offers to do the Sporting Article for half price.

"7. He also offers to find his own punctuation.

"8. He candidly admits that he does not know much about horses; but he says that, at any rate, he knows more than *you* !

"9. Shall I close with this young person, Nicholas?

"10. Or, will you send me your copy?"

As for the signature, Sir, where it says "yours affectionately," I look upon such, under the circumstances, as being little better than a delusive mockery.

There have been several reasons why NICHOLAS did not send you his copy. In the first place I have been sitting up with a sick friend, but I have been also confined to my home by acute rheumatism, and have likewise had for to go out a good deal into society. As to sending for the salary, why not? I cannot conceive, my dear young Friend, for such I hold you still, a happier position than that of a man of letters who gets his money regular, whether he does his work or quite the contrary.

Far be it from me, Sir, to disturb an arrangement so satisfactory.

Perhaps you will be so good enough as to tell the young man he may walk.

Congratulating us all on the termination of another volume of the New Serious—and I think, Sir, that on all such occasions the proprietors might give us a handsome bonus all around, I am, Sir, so no more at present from NICHOLAS.

P.S. 2.—My literary man says the mottoes he has chosen are peculiarly appropriate. Personally, I think as they are rather vulgar and censorious, but I will not venture to set up my own opinion against Shakespeare, who was himself, I believe, a sportive writer, and therefore called (by way of joke) "the Fancy's child," just as NICHOLAS might figuratively be spoken of as "a Kid of the Turf."

NICHOLAS MORALISES WITH REGARD TO HIS FAVOURITE PURSUIT.

"A gentle answer did the Old Man make."—*Wordsworth.*
Resolution and Independence.

BELGRAVIA.

ON THE INSTABILITY OF HUMAN AFFAIRS.

It is said by a writer in a daily contemporary under the signature of "Asmodeus" (which I have some reason to believe as it is a fictitious name), "that he would be the last to speak ill of the dead, but there is a peculiar moral in the fact that last week a bookmaker died who was making a £5000 book on the Derby, and now it transpires that the deceased had not enough capital to defray his own funeral expenses!"

Now, my dear young Friend, it is exaggerative in "Asmodeus" to say as he would be the last man to speak ill of the dead, for NICHOLAS would be laster still; but the event, my dear young Friend, is calculated to make us all reflect how mutable we are! Do I blame the bookmaker? No, Sir, and I will tell you why. I have been pretty much in the same position myself—not meaning that I ever died without leaving enough to pay my funeral expenses, for you would not believe me, even if I were to swear it, but I have made a book for never you mind how many thousands, at a time when a five-pound note was an article which the Prophet seldom saw, and never touched. Sir, I *won!* Thanks to my ingenuity and enterprise, I potted a heap of money—and, as you know, have since become one of the Leviathans of the Turf, wallowing in riches and in the respectful admiration of my fellow-man. Suppose, however, I had happened to *lose?*

Sir, in that melancholy event, the form of NICHOLAS would not for many weeks have been distinctly visible to the naked eye, like the recent eclipse—at any rate, not on *this* side of the English Channel. A melancholy, but still handsome old Bird, so to speak, would have been observed to alight on a foreign shore at Bolong, and perhaps to wing its way to some "*hay-stamina*," as the French call a house of refreshment, just as if it was a feed for horses; the old Bird in question might probably have had a pair of blue spectacles fixed across my beak; but to the children of Britannia, my dear young Friend, and especially to all those Sportive men of merry, merry England with whom he had any pecuniary transactions, NICHOLAS would have been "non est" —and although the Poet (than whom I do not think much of him, he often making the most deceptive and ridicolas remarks) observes that "a non-est man's the noblest work of God," yet NICHOLAS is still inclined to doubt whether such would have been the general opinion of the Prophet's conduct, whether at Tattersall's, Bride Lane, or the Ruins.

But, my dear young Friend, do not let us all be a set of canting humbugs! If you say that a betting-man who incurs liabilities which he cannot meet—who makes bets, in fact, entirely on the basis of credit—if you say, Sir, that such a man is only one step from a Swindler, then I say you are harsh. Be honest, my young Friend; speak the plain truth; say that he is only one step from a Railway Financier; and NICHOLAS, with a blush that ever he should have fell so low, will sorrowfully own that right you are.

All I ask, Sir, on behalf of self and other gentlemen of the same profession, is this: *Tar us all with the same*

Brush! I have done some queer things in my time, as, perhaps, you will believe; but I never created fictitious capital to the extent of a million, and thereby robbed the widow and the orphan. *I never had the chance!*

NICHOLAS.

P.S.—I think it is just as well for the widow and orphan that I had *not*.

With regard to the University Boat Race, I have had a vision. *It will be won, this year, by Cambridge.* I am sorry for ye, ye gallant young Oxtabs; but ye must remember as it is long since the Cantabonians have had a turn.

NICHOLAS.

P.S.—I have found a chapter or two of my " Knurr and Spell," just the rough draft, so to speak. Perhaps we had better print even this than seem to break faith with the public? Not as the public would hesitate to break faith with you or me. *I* know the public, my dear young Friend!

PASSAGES FROM THE DIARY OF AN OLD ENGLISH GENTLEMAN.

> I feel within my aged breast,
> A power that will not be repressed;
> It prompts my voice, it swells my veins,
> It burns, it maddens, it constrains !
> SCOTT.—" Lord of the Isles."

" Oh, my Prophetic soul, my "—Relative!—SHAKESPEARE.

BELGRAVIA.

Saturday, 30th March. Had an interview with my Gentleman of the Press, and which he furnished me with the motto I have just wrote down. *It is full short;* but the respectability of its being one of Scott's lot makes amend, though I rather forget where it was as "Lord of the Isles" was made a favourite. As to "swelling my veins," a man is only too apt to feel so if he have been out late the night before. *Memorandum.* To write to my Young Friend and tell him as "Lecturer" is safe for to win the Northamptonshire Stakes on Tuesday.

Tuesday night, 2*nd April.* Result. If my hand trembles as I write it down, it is not through drink. I wish it was! I wish there was nothing *worse* than Drink!!! What's the matter? *Ruin's* the matter!

GREAT NORTHAMPTONSHIRE STAKES.

Quick March	...	...	...	...	1
Amanda colt	...	...	...	...	2
Lecturer	...	...	...	...	3

Smashed again, by all that's vexatious! Knocked over—bowled clean out,—me, NICHOLAS, a man as have known the turf for years,—and all by a rank outsider!! Another blow like this will make the Prophet *non est.* The only consolation is that I acted truthful and fair by my Young Friend, and did not involve him in my own misfortunes.

Wednesday morning, 3*rd April.* Back again in Belgravia, but I do not think as I shall be able to stay here long. It have already got about as I have had misfortunes; and on coming up in the train, who should I see but my loathsome and low-lived Relative, perhaps the only man on the course as had backed "Quick March," and which he openly derided of me. As for the game little "Lecturer," here is wishing as he was boiled alive—the brute! NICHOLAS.

P.S.—I shall try and bring myself round again all right by backing Cambridge for the University Boat Race.

NICHOLAS IN THE DUMPS.

"Back!"—SHAKESPEARE.

MY DEAR YOUNG FRIEND,—Misfortune jolly soon oozes out as you will see as my Gentleman of the Press have already turned against me, he only providing me with a single word for a motto out of old Shakespeare, and which it is all very well for poets to say "Back," but suppose you *have* backed, and the luck have gone against you, and your credit beginning to be shy? There is no knowing how human affairs will turn out, and the Prophet *may* yet pull himself square on coming events; but, my dear young man, I will not disguise it from you that NICHOLAS have lost, and heavily.

The course of NICHOLAS, thank goodness, is tolerably clear. If fortune should again declare against him, he will be quite willing to go over to Paris for you, my dear young Friend, and continue in your employment by writing of Art-Criticisms for you on the Exhibition, he knowing quite as much about it as some which are employed at home by your serious contempories. The Prophet thinks that a series of light and homorous articles on "Eating Horseflesh: by One who knows better than for to do so," might be quite a feature, Sir, in your otherwise well-conducted journal. Or, I might see, perhaps, whether I happen to have left the MS. of my "Knurr and Spell" behind me during one of my passing visits to the gay capital of our lively neighbours. In any case, Sir, I trust as you will remember former

services, and not turn a poor, ruinous old man out on
the streets, which I am nobody's enemy but my own,
and have been known to keep steady for weeks together.   Besides, Sir, I am no worse than my prophetic
rivals, which have all been let in the hole this season ;
and I am still confident, Gentlemen, as my luck will
come back when the weather gets a little warmer,
NICHOLAS being firmly of opinion that hitherto the East
wind have got into his head.   Rally round the old
adviser, NICHOLAS !   Who sent you the Derby winner
of 1865 ?   Who sent you the Derby winner of 1866 ?
Who sent you the absolute first, second, and third for
the '67 St. Leger ?   Trust to the Prophet !   Rally round
him !!   And all will yet be joy !!!

NICHOLAS.

P.S.—I have ventured to draw on you for a few
weeks' salary in advance, and got it cashed in the
City.

P.S. 2.—I do not think it necessary to send my
present address.

NICHOLAS AT THE BOAT RACE.

"Row, Brothers, Row!"—Popular Song.
"Here's a jolly row!"—Popular Saying.

SHEERNESS.

RESPECTED SIR,—My Gentleman of the Press having
left me in the lurch, and than whom a more ungrateful
scoundrel, NICHOLAS having always treated him as an
equal, and many is the glass of sherry-wine which he
have had at my expense, though always giving himself
airs and I daresay a deuced deal fonder of boozing along
with his Spensers and Wordsworths than of mixing in

respectable society, so, Respected Sir, for such I have ever held you, my Gentleman of the Press having left me in the lurch, I have drawn upon my own reading and observation for the mottoes of the present week, and which I consider as they are a deal more to the purpose than the far-fetched allusions of my literary man and his lot. I hate anything far-fetched, and always did, especially beer. And when I say as I have drawn upon my own reading and observation, I must not forget to apologise, the luck having gone against me, for having likewise drawn upon *you*, as mentioned in last week's countrybution to your New Serious.

But, Respected Sir, from *you* also I consider as an explanation is required. After the years I have served you, was it just—was it grateful—was it worthy of a fine old English gentleman, one of the holden time, chorus —like a fine old English gentleman, one of the holden time—for to throw me over quite so public and so quick? And when NICHOLAS says, "throw me over," he do not mean it in a literal sense, as if you had seized the Prophet by the scruff of his neck, which you would have been quite justified in doing, Sir, and shied him into the Thames last Saturday, for *that* could only have been a gentlemanly though violent evolution of tempory anger, NICHOLAS having cost you pounds and pounds by his unfortunate tip for the interesting aquatical computation; no, my dear young Friend—if such you will still kindly allow me to call you—nor yet do I complain because you thought proper to cut me dead on Barnes Terrace, for I will admit as the old man, through looking flushed with the morning air, and not being used to taking spirituous liquors so early in the day, and which I only did so under advice, there being several betting-men along with me, all of which may easily have conveyed the erroneous impression that NICHOLAS was more of a low lot than of a fine old English gentleman as before mentioned, and less calculated for to deliver a temperance oration than for to be took up by the police. Please begin another sentence, my worthy and estimable printers, if such you will still allow me to call you ; and should the Prophet ever have given you unnecessary trouble along of his authorgraphy and pointuation, he hopes you will not be too hard on an old man when he's down.

No, Sir ; but what I venture respectfully to complain of—and what, if circumstances were different, I should freely say as it was a scandalous shame—is, that on Saturday afternoon you exhibited a placard in your office window, near the casts of the scientific animals, as follows :—

Oxford and Cambridge Boat Race.

—

THE OLD MAN WRONG AGAIN!

[*See* FUN.

See "FUN," forsooth! I am glad as you do so. I don't. I call it depreciating of the property, and crying stinking fish, saving your presence. Why, if you *must* have a flaming poster on the subject, and which I do not myself see the necessity, it is my honest conviction as a better one could have been drawn up by the office-boy, if he will still allow me to call him so. Depend upon it, Sir, if you had only brazened it out, the public would soon have got muddled in his head as usual. I know the public quite as well as the public knows *me;* and I should say, Sir, as it was scarcely possible for any two parties to respect each other less! No, Sir, *here's my notion :—*

Oxford and Cambridge Boat Race.

RIGHT AGAIN! TRIUMPH OF NICHOLAS!

Who sent you the Absolute Second?

[*See* FUN.

You will see, Sir, as I have changed my address. Several reasons have induced me for to go out of town, especially climate. I find that London was getting rather too warm—in fact, if I may say so, too hot to hold me; and so, having had a very kind invitation from a country friend which knowed me when I was respectable, years and years ago, and thinking as Sheerness was a tolerably secluded spot, down I came; but when I reached this happy village, the friend of my infancy, which had lost heavy on the Light Blue by following my tip, he raised his unhallowed hands against me, and let me have it hot upon my hi. We are now reconciled, and if Plaudit wins the Two Thousand, or the game little Lecturer wins the Chester Cup, I shall come back, otherwise it is more than probable as I shall keep out of the way.

P.S. 2.—The sherry wine here is beastly. You *might* send me down some.

P.S. 3.—I have a good thing for the Derby.

NICHOLAS.

NICHOLAS DOWN UPON HIS LUCK.

"Down, down, hey derry down!"—*Popular Song.*
"Down among the dead men let him lie!"—*Popular Chorus.*
"All in the Downs!"—*Popular Ballad.*
Epsom Downs.—*Popular Race-Course.*

HORSELAYDOWN.

HONOURED AND RESPECTED SIR,—Considerable surprise have been expressed at the absence of NICHOLAS from your columns in the last number of the New Serious, and which I have no doubt but what such must have inflicted a bitter pang of disappointment on many thousands of the public breasts.

Considerable surprise have also been expressed, in the commercial circles of Belgravia, at the absence of NICHOLAS from his home for a protracted period, during which all attempts to extort money from the Old Man, no matter how ingenious the plea or plausible the pretext, have been, and will be so, entirely futile that it is the odds of the National Debt to a midshipman's half-pay, as they will not get a single sixpence out of NICHOLAS until his circumstances are very, very different.

You may remember, dear Sir, that the Prophet vaticinated the victory of Cambridge over Oxford in the aquatical computation on the Thames ;—in fact, as you probably lost money by backing my selection, it is more than likely, as the fact may still be vividly impressed upon your mind—a mind, Sir, than which I may truly say none more cultivated and vivacious, if so much so.

It may also, dear Sir, be within your affable recollection that Nicholas prophesied Plaudit for the Two Thousand, and stuck to him with a consistency which be do not often exhibit with regard to any public animal whatever.

Nor, my dear and venerated benefactor, is it likely as you have forgotten that, several weeks ago, I unhesitatingly declared that the Chester Cup would be won by the game little Lecturer.

Perhaps, as it is highly desirable we should arrive at some clear and definite understanding, I had better put the matter into a tabular form, and if such causes any additional trouble to your worthy printers, than whom I am sure, if so much so.   .   .   .   .   .   .

EVENTS.	SELECTIONS OF NICHOLAS.	ACTUAL WINNERS.
Oxford and Cambridge	Cambridge.	Oxford.
Two Thousand Guineas	Plaudit.	Vauban.
Chester Cup...............	Lecturer.	Beeswing.

If some of your contemporaries, Sir, would act with equal candour, it might be good for the public, though bad for the prophets.

Well, no man can stand three such facers in such quick succession. After hovering about—especially at Sheerness, which I will say a word or two about it presently—I came back into the old neighbourhood of Bermondsey. Mrs. Cripps, would, I daresay, have been delighted, for many reasons, to behold her once-loved lodger; but, as one of those many reasons is that there is still a little pecuniary trifle outstanding between us, I have curbed my natural anxiety for to visit her. Horselaydown, however, is in the immediate vicinity; besides being near the River Thames, so that by taking a wherry I could quickly cross from one county to another, if a set of malignant creditors should really push the Prophet hard. Besides, I shall be in a favourable position for picking up aquatic intelligence, to which I feel that you have not hitherto done justice in your otherwise well-conducted periodical publication.

NICHOLAS.

NICHOLAS IN BUSINESS FOR HIMSELF.

THE ORIENTAL REPOSITORY, HORSELAYDOWN.

MY DEAR YOUNG FRIEND,—To all those which may have inquired, some of them individuously, and others in the spirit of a brother man, concerning of my present *locus in quo* you are now in a position to reply that I may be found at the above address, where all the chief periodicals of the day are on sale, and the *Times* lent to read. I was absent from your cheerful columns last week, it is true; but, my dear young Friend, your classic lore will remind you as Rome was not built in a day, nor yet was the Oriental Repository, which I had to take it with some of the old stock, and between ourselves it has got a bad name, or they would not let me have it cheap. Your artist, however—than whom a more respectable young man for his position in life, and I wish I had had something better on the premises at the moment than half of a bottle of stout which, I am afraid, as it was a little turned with the hot weather—your artist, Sir, will tell you that NICHOLAS, who was once the glass of fashion, the mould of form, and the cynicsure of neighbouring eyes, is quietly converted into an honest British tradesman, ever ready for to sell you a penny Sunday paper, affable to the widow and the orphan, and not unlikely for to ultimately soar into the very loftiest parochial honours.

You will naturally ask me where I got my capital. I got it, my dear young Friend, from the quarter where least expected. At a time when my frenzied appeals to *you*, Sir, for a ten-pound note was treated with derision—and, between ourselves, you would never have seen the money again if you had been fool enough to lend it!—at that time, Sir, who should come forward but my Relative, of whom I have frequently spoken in these pages, not always, perhaps, with that warm affection which it is his rightful due, but well he knows as I have always really loved him. His words were plain and blunt, which I will transcribe a few of them : " If left without any assistance whatever, you will probably take to Crime; and, although you have treated your best friends with scandalous ingratitude, they have no desire to see you in a felon's cell. You shall have another chance. You are not absolutely a fool ; and with common care and attention you may pick up a decent living in the periodical line. Stick to business ; keep yourself sober ; and all may yet be well." Very plainly put, Sir, was it not ? and so here is my Relative's jolly good health, in a bumper! And *yours*, Sir! And we will let the bumper pass, whilst we'll fill another glass, to the athletic men of merry, merry England !

"The Oriental Repository," Sir, it is a name, or rather an appellation, which I have invented it all out of my own head, on account of Horselaydown being in the East.

THE DERBY OF 1867.

From the spirited delineation, Sir, given by your Artist, the public will see as I had not fallen into a

Prophetic Trance, but was a-standing at my shop door, with all my wits about me, and a leary smile upon those lineaments which, although at present confined chiefly to the neighbourhood of the Oriental Repository (for fiscal reasons), were once familiar to Britannia's Hope and all the rest of the Aristocracy. It was on one of the few warm days with which we have been favoured. The Old Man's heart, Sir, was full. The manly conduct of his Relative had touched him a good deal. He had likewise been having a little rum-and-water with a sea-captain. At such a moment, Sir, it is not unlikely as the prophetic spirit may have stirred me to my inmost depths. As usual on such occasions, it took a metrical form.

> Awake, Prophetic Harp! In Sixty-five
> You sent them Gladiateur, who's still alive;
> In Sixty-six was NICHOLAS a dolt,
> Sending Lord Lyon and the Bribery Colt?
> Gents, get your money ready, fair and free,
> While the Old Man proclaims One, Two, and Three!

So you see, I begin it as cocky as possible—though between ourselves I cannot hope to be successful *every* year.

> First in the line of sight appears Vauban,
> One of the boldest as has ever ran;
> Yes, just as I have written long ago,
> Look, the " Rake's Progress " has resulted so.
> I've pledged myself to eat him should he win,
> But didn't say when feeding would begin;
> And it would prove, Sir, an unpleasant dinner
> For to devour a real " dead " Derby winner!
> If D'Estournel his temper keep, no horse
> Can match him on the trying Epsom course.
> Van Amburgh, too, will earn a lasting fame, or
> *Not* be described as a Lord Lyon-tamer !

Say, say ! is Hermit always in the dark ?
Or will the Marksman never hit the mark ?
Will mighty Julius struggle still in vain ?
Nor Plaudit come unto the front again ?
Perpend these hints ; their hidden meaning scan,
And, if ye win, send stamps to the Old Man ;
The minimum it will be half-a-crown,
At the Oriental Repository, Horselaydown !

NICHOLAS.

P.S.—Do not forget, "The Oriental Repository," Horselaydown. All works on Knurr and Spell kept in stock. Soda-water sold.

The Oriental Repository, Horselaydown (Limited).

"I will be Correspondent to command,
And do my spiriting gently."

SHAKESPEARE. Ariel: *Tempest.*

(Routledge's Shilling Edition is kept in stock at the Repository.)

Immense Success of Nicholas, and Brilliant Triumph of the Old Man!

N.B.—Mr. Nicholas is not in the habit of resorting to this method of advertisement, but is compelled to do so on the present occasion by a regard for the interests and feelings of his brother directors of the Repository, where periodicals may be ordered a fortnight in advance.

My dear young Friend, Fellow-Sportsman, and Brother-Winner,—The heart of the Old Man is full. Since that happy morning when you and me, Sir, talked it over in the back office, with nobody present but a large white cat and the fine old artist which have drawn my portrait—since we agreed that the tip should

be Hermit, Marksman, and Vauban, the only gloomy
feelings in the Prophet's bosom have been two—one
that he had not the wealth of Creases for to back his
selection, the other that perhaps we did not make it
altogether quite so plain to the public as might have
been desired.   For that fault, however,—if fault it were,
—I decline to hold myself responsible.   It's *your* business, my young Friend, for to edit the paper and put
things in proper order; and if, through not being much
of a sportive character—nor do I believe as you really
know a racer from a radish—you mix up the horses'
names which are sent you in accordance with your own
crotchetty whims, or the suggestions of the printers,
which have been a deal too free of late with the Prophet's
copy—if you then mislead the fine old artist likewise,
after he have drawn for you for the last fifty years, and
get him to put Hermit second when I distinctly wrote,
having the memorandum by me, and excuse haste of
spelling—" you put the Hermit fust, symbolifixing him
by a old cove rather down upon his luck, and with none
too much clothes for to wear "—if thus you act, the
blame is not justly due to NICHOLAS.

Happily, however, for the interests of truth and
justice, *literary scriptures manent* (Latin quotations kept
in stock at the Repository), and my own poetic words
will vindicate me with the public.   I was fair, I was
more than fair, to Vauban, and I take no shame for it.
I said he was

> " One of the boldest as has ever ran ; "

and so he was, a good game horse.   I then treated a
few others with that happy mixture of good-humour
and sarcasm which is now known throughout an empire

on which the sun never sets as NICHOLASTIC; and having done so, I bust so to speak—not as I mean your Prophet really flew asunder, with his head flying wildly into the air, like the cork of the soda-water bottle—and he keeps it in stock at the Repository—but I bust into this distinct and powerful prophecy:—

> "Say, say, is Hermit always in the dark,
> And will the Marksman never hit the mark?"

THUS BRACKETING TOGETHER THE ABSOLUTE FIRST AND SECOND !!!

As for my Relative, I have no particular complaint for to make against him just at present. I dare say as he means well, and if he is far indeed from being a gentleman and scholar, most of his friends going so far as to say he is a mean old hunks, why we cannot make a silk purse out of the ear of a female swine. He have recently been of great service to NICHOLAS, and so you see I stand up for him.

Me and some other gentlemen are a-turning of the Repository into a Company, which I daresay more will be heard of it. By Order of the Board,

NICHOLAS, Managing Director.

P.S.—Do not forget the Oriental Repository (Limited), Horselaydown. The Old Man always at home, or may be found at the " Grapes," where the best of sherry wine. Lessons given in Knurr and Spell. Portraits of NICHOLAS, from a crown. Rats.

NICHOLAS ON COMMERCIAL PURSUITS, THE INFLUENCE OF THE TURF, AND MORALITY.

THE ORIENTAL REPOSITORY (LIMITED), HORSELAYDOWN.

MY DEAR YOUNG FRIEND,—Your favour of yesterday's date is duly to hand, and contents noted.

Excuse me if you find my style a little cramped to what it were. The fact is that in the conduct of an immense business like the Oriental Repository, I naturally lose a good deal of my old littery gaiety and fall back upon a more commercial method of expression. As one of London's merchant princes—and which I have quite as much right to the title as any ordinary Lord Mayor, such being generally rather in the way of wholesale trade than what my friends, Baring Brothers, would understand by the word commerce—as one of London's merchant princes, and having to go into the City early of a morning for to get our stock of papers, and which the way that the boys chaff an elderly man is fiendish—as one of London's merchant princes, the business steadily increasing and the branch which I have set up at Sheerness already returning me a handsome profit, NICHOLAS being at last recognised in his native town as a true local Reformer, and if the inhabitants have any sense of gratitude they will send the Old Man a testimonial, either something capable (like himself) of holding a good deal of liquor, or else (which he would prefer) a purse of sovereigns—as one of London's merchant princes—

NICHOLAS have been advised by his Relative to abandon the Turf altogether, and stick to his shop; but well do I know that this is only his envy, he being (though a good fellow in his way), always jealous of my superior abilities and my more aristocratical bearing.

NICHOLAS have no patience, my dear young friend, with this here outcry all of a sudden against the Turf. We are told that the Turf ain't respectable. Why, in the name of Ruff's Guide and the Racing Calendar, *who ever thought it was?*

Young noblemen, we are told, go to the bad. It is a great pity, of course; but if a boy happens to be a profligate and a fool, how on earth are you to prevent him from squandering his estate and dishonouring his name?

I am not myself connected with the Peerage, though my family have always (until my own time) been considered respectable, and an ancestor of mine, as I have often told you, was formerly in the Custom House itself; but supposing me to be a duke, do you think as I could not have ruined myself by other ways than betting on the Turf? Supposing as I was the Duke of Horselaydown in the peerage of England, and the Duke of Mac Nichol in the peerage of Scotland, and Le Duc de Nicholas in the peerage of France—and supposing I was, at the same time, a queer sort, do you think as it is race-horses alone which would lead me—and *that* pretty quick—to the mischief? Oh no, ye canst not think so. The simple truth is that when a man is a bad egg, it don't much matter what spoon you crack him with.

If you come to mere morality, mind you, the Old Man is not sure as you are a bit worse, you young men of 1867, than what he was himself at an anollogus period, he being accustomed for to carry on dreadful; and many is the officer of police which might even now recognise in the weather-worn countenance of NICHOLAS some resemblance to one who in formal years—but perhaps this is vanity-glorious.

The peculiarity of young men just now—and in saying young men, the Prophet means from twenty to
thirty, leaving out boys on the one side and steady old
coves on the other—the peculiarity of young men just
now is that they care for little and believe in nothing.
In NICHOLAS'S own time, even when a youngster was
vicious, there was generally two things about him as
was worth notice:—in the first place, he got something
like enjoyment out of his vices; and in the second
place he was seldom so far gone but what he was
ashamed of them.

Young Hopeful of the present day still talks about
seeing life; but you would think as it was Death he
saw, his eyes get so dull and fixed. Enjoyment, Sir?
You come along of NICHOLAS to any place where they
congregate, these young men; and your good and gifted
old guide, Sir, meaning me, will turn round upon you
with the majesty of a Socrates or even a Plater, and bid
ye answer whether ever in your life you saw faces more
dull, more weary, more woebegone. They *have* ate their
cake, these boys; and not only can they consequently
never have such again, but it have made them far from
well in their insides.

[These remarks may seem harsh; but, Sir, the
patience of Job himself would have changed to the
indignant ferocity of an irritated Bradlaugh, had certain
events befallen him.

*Every penny made in the Repository has been dropped
at Ascot!* There; *now* the murder's out. *Now*, perhaps,
you perceive why the Prophet, usually so gay, is at
present much less like an exulting Spirit of Joy than
what he is like a bear with a sore head, and has serious
thoughts of cutting the whole concern, never reading

another sportive paper, never writing another sportive prophecy, but taking my Relative's hint and seriously sticking to business, until I shall have realized enough to resume my old pursoots.]

And now, Sir, about manners. They are not ashamed, these young ones are not, to behave in a way which NICHOLAS—though he do not like the word—is constrained to call "caddish." I am not myself of noble blood, though my family is respectable and always looks back with pride to the illustrious traditions of those grand old days when one of us was connected with Britannia's Custom House itself; but I should be sorry such as I am, to behave in the way that is now common —I should just say as it *was* common, in a parenthesis ! —amongst our young men, not merely amongst those who are fast, and consequently loose, but even amongst steadier ones.

There is a growing indifference to the claims of woman, Sir, which is a sign of barbarical deterioration— Young England puffs tobacco, Sir, in her face ; he talks to her about subjects, the very mention of which is an insult for which an honest girl's brother would be quite justified in knocking him down ; the gentle courtesy of the past is dead ; and with the exception of a few cavaliers *de la vieille roche*—such as NICHOLAS himself— society is getting like a Cremorne with all the amusements left out.

These remarks, Sir, have been suggested to the Prophet by incidents which happened to him recently in Paris, where he thought himself justified, being still a bachelor, in a little flirtation with a young lady at Spiers and Pond's, and which the fair one and him was getting along as nicely as possible, when who should step in but a young whipper-snapper, than whom I am sure his hat was only fit for a show, and as for his coat—well, the Prophet would not advise him for to show himself to his schoolmaster in such, since the temptation might be too many for that pedagogue—and which I could plainly hear him calling of me "a pottering old tout;" *and she laughed at* NICHOLAS !

NICHOLAS ON BRITISH HOSPITALITY.
ORIENTAL REPOSITORY (LIMITED), HORSELAYDOWN.

MY DEAR YOUNG FRIEND,—My relative, who is not a fool, whatever else he may be, have suggested that remarks of a vaticinatory and even prophetic character might be applied to many other events besides those which are mixed up with my country's Turf; and he have hinted that, at my time of life, NICHOLAS has a right to express his own opinion on any subject in the world, bar none.

NICHOLAS have been requested for to lend his powerful and world-wide aid on behalf of British Hospitality to our Belgian visitors. The Old Man cannot say that he knows very much about the Belgians, nor yet about Belgia itself, he having only been there once, nor do you find him so again. No, no, my brave young Belgic visitors; never no more will the Prophet cross the stormy ocean, except it be to Paris direct. NICHOLAS, however, is bound to say that when he *was* in Belgia, he was treated with sumptuous hospitality and champagne wine all day; and NICHOLAS has great pleasure in coming forward, alongside of H.R.H. and the noblest of the land, to vindicate his country's character for hospitality.

His country's character for hospitality ain't good.

NICHOLAS will not pretend to know much about geography and the use of globes, though I will yield to no man of my age and weight, bar none, in estimating of the points of the horse; but NICHOLAS have been reading a good deal in the papers at the Repository, and rumours have reached him concerning of Pashas of Turkey (where Constantinople is, as the song was wrote about), and the Sultans of the Egyptians, and other monarchs, all of whom are likely for to visit Britain's shore.

Gentlemen all, I have noticed that now these illustrious visitors are coming we don't know what to do with them.

It is easy enough—though mean—to let 'em all take lodgings at a respectable public, if any such will admit the heathen; but some kind of State notice ought to be taken of 'em, and something done for to improve their minds. Accordingly,

NICHOLAS WILL GIVE THE EASTERN POTENTATES
A free Admission
To VIEW THE ORIENTAL REPOSITORY, (LIMITED).

And, my dear young Friend, representing—as you do on this auspicious and momentous occasion—the tax-paying public of Great Britain, I am sure that you will only be too delighted for to make good any little expense to which I may be put.

Nor is even this the full extent of British Hospitality. NICHOLAS is prepared for to go further still and to give

AN INTERNATIONAL SOIREE.
Programme.
7 p.m.—March to Horselaydown by the Belgian

Volunteers.   N.B.—Any of the Belgian Volunteers as
may like to bring their own provisions will be allowed
to do so.

8. p.m.—Opening of the Oriental Repository.

8.15 p.m.—Arrival of the Belgians, Egyptians, Tur-
keys, and Abbeysinias.   N.B.—Any monarchs liking to
come in their own carriages will be allowed for to do
so.   Gentlemen, the Repository is Liberty Hall!
Should any King prefer the threepenny 'bus, he will be
entitled for to receive back his fare on producing, at the
Repository, a stamped receipt from the conductor—
but NICHOLAS truly hopes that no foreign monarch will
be quite so mean.

8.20 p.m.—Anybody anxious to present purses to
NICHOLAS will be allowed to do so.

8.30 p.m.—Public Opening of Two Bottles of Sherry
Wine.   N.B.—The corks will be Inaugurated by Sir
Wentworth Dilke and Mr. Henry Cole, C.B.

8.35 p.m.—The Prophet will declare that the sherry
wine *is* open.   N.B.—This will be considered as equiva-
lent to a good deal.

8.36 p.m.—The foreign Visitors will begin to wonder what it all means.   Observing which, at exactly

8.37 p.m.—NICHOLAS will offer the Sultan a tumbler
of sherbet.   Great enthusiasm.   No charge will be made
for the sherbet.

9 p.m.—The Belgians will be allowed to send for
what they like in the way of liquor.   No charge will be
made for this permission.

10 p.m.—The Old Man will make a gracious valedictory address, ending with the words, " Don't you think
you'd better go?"   Greater enthusiasm than ever.
The ceremony will then conclude by NICHOLAS singing

the National Anthem in the back parlour; and the character of British Hospitality will THUS be redeemed!   NICHOLAS.

NICHOLAS ON THE RECENT FESTIVITIES.

MY DEAR YOUNG FRIEND,—Had I the arms of a Briareus, or even of a Morpheus, combined with the eyes of an Argus (by whom I do not mean the sportive correspondent of the *Morning Post*, though here is wishing him no harm)—and if you were likewise for to endow the Old Man with as many legs as used to meet in the Ruins, it would still be utterly impossible for NICHOLAS to cope with the rush of events, all demanding of either sportive or prophetic treatment.

NICHOLAS AND THE BELGIANS.

(From the Prophet's own Penny-a-liner.)

Considerable excitement was recently occasioned not a hundred miles from the neighbourhood of the Oriental Repository, kept by the well-known MR. NICHOLAS, in Horselaydown, by the appearance of a large number of the Belgian Volunteers. From circumstances which have since transpired, it is fully believed that had an alarming conflagration broken out at this moment, the flames would have lit up in bright relief the steeples of the neighbouring religious edifices, and that much praise would also have been due to the police for keeping off the pressure of the crowd. Fortunately, the devouring element was otherwise employed.

[Note by NICHOLAS.—Of course it was. There was a dinner at the Mansion House. *That's* the place that really stood in danger from the "devouring" element,

not the Repository, where it is but little as I eat, goodness knows.   Go on with the account now, Messrs.
Printers and Co.]

On arriving at the Oriental Repository—a spacious
building in no particular order of architecture—the
Belgians were most warmly received by their enter-
tainer, who addressed them in the French language
with great fluency, and which, when it was interpreted
to them, they expressed themselves much pleased with
his truly intro-national sentiments.   The distinguished
host stated his regret that he could not entertain them
all at once; but added, that if they would go round to
the " Admiral Keppel " in three distinct bodies, he would
personally accompany each detachment, and make sure
that the liquor was good by tasting it himself.

This proposition being received with enthusiastic
cheers, the first distinct body set out upon its march,
accompanied by NICHOLAS and your Reporter.   The
proceedings at the " Admiral Keppel" were of a very
satisfactory kind—very satisfactory kind—especially
the rum-and-water.

The second distinct body was equally fortunate, and
the proceedings at the " Admiral Keppel " were still
satisfactory—still *most* satisfactory—and where is he
who can deny such, especially the whiskey-toddy?
And where is he who can deny whiskey-toddy?   But
it made the Belgians as tight—as—a—drum, you know
—tightsadrum.   Me and old NICHOLAS, being used to it,
wasn't even touched—even touched.   But you *should*
have seen the *third* distinct body.   Why, they were
twice as numerous as the others; and not a man of 'em
sober, except me and old NICHOLAS, in the third distinct
—distinctive body.

[Note by NICHOLAS.—The account, allowing for a little exaggeration, is substantially correct; but where it says that *he* wasn't "even touched," why, I had—being a householder—to bail him out!]

NICHOLAS.

NICHOLAS AT GOODWOOD.

BRIGHTON, SOUTH COAST.

MY DEAR YOUNG FRIEND,—It is all of no use. Me and the Turf were made for one another, and we cannot be long divided. Business at the Repository would have got along tolerably well, I dare say, if I could have consented for to put my Pegasus in harness—and would back that animal, weight for age, against any other Pegasuses of the time, bar none; if I could have cramped my soaring aspirations, bottled up my ardent love for good society, and sunk to the level of a retail trader.

It was not to be. I *did* think of going in for civic honours at one time, but I am told as the Common Council is a low lot; and the sale of newspapers over a counter, my dear young Friend, although it may have tendencies for to improve the mind and such, yet it is very trying when the boys come in of a morning, and begin for to chivy you, so for to speak, than whom I am sure as one of them called me a blear-eyed old leg, which is not merely insulting, but anatomically impossible.

The Repository, however, has its uses. Between ourselves, of course, Betting-houses have been long abolished, by the strong arm of the law; oh certainly, yes, my dear young Friend; and quite right, too.

Betting, as we all know, is immoral—ain't it, Sir? Twig?

There are lists at the Repository, gentlemen all; and the market rates strictly observed. You may trust Mr. Nicholas with any amount. He pledges himself for to let you to do so—and when he says "pledges himself" he do not mean as he is in the habit of putting himself up the spout when in tempory embarrassment, but like signing your name when you write to a newspaper, "as a guarantee of good faith."

The advent, Sir, of glorious Goodwood brought matters to a crisis. Your aged man shut up the Repository for a day or two—several deposits having been made there—and he rigged himself up with the funds thus obtained in a style which, he flatters himself, was tolerably "down the road." When you are a public character you must manage to keep up appearances. Personally, I am more remarkable for intellect than what I am for beauty, though still a good-looking old chap for my period, if I may say so without being vanity-glorious, and have never been done justice by the artises, they always representing Nicholas as though he had been partaking of too much for to drink.

But oh, my dear young Friend, what trials awaited my proud spirit! I was once, as you are well aware, hand-in-hand with my country's youthful aristocracy, than whom I am sure a finer set of young fellows, though a little gay; but the noblemen and gents which gladly fraternised with Mr. Nicholas the eminent Turfite, would have nothing for to say to Mr. Nicholas the honest retail Trader, and the proprietor of a Repository than which I am sure anything more truly an emporium.

H.R.H. himself—my once bosom friend—still gave me a friendly nod as I lifted off my hat : but the Cambridges never noticed me at all, nor yet did Teck.

This comes, Sir, of being lured by wily relatives into compromising of my position as a gentleman on the Turf, and a man, one of whose ancestors was under Government in the Custom House itself—compromising of my position, Sir, and entering into trade. For it is, after all, Sir, a satisfactory thing to a man who loves his country, that princes and nobles will have nothing to say to traders, such as merchants and Repositorians ; but that they will sit down with betting-men, and hob and nob with money-lenders, and smoke with trainers, and slap boy-jockeys on the back as they ply them with champagne.

I think, my dear young Friend, as I shall have for to cut the shop, and get back into society.

NICHOLAS.

P.S.—I am stopping here at a very comfortable hotel, and which I have told them as I am your Representative, and they will send the bill to the office accordingly.

NICHOLAS AT THE SEASIDE.

THE CLIFFS OF ALBION.

MY DEAR YOUNG FRIEND,—You will see by the above address as I have begun for to take my holidays, feeling sure as you would wish me for to do so about this period, although, from feelings of delicacy towards the other contributors, you have nobly abstained from telling me so to my face. Between ourselves, it was high time as I gave myself a little rest and recreation. The cares of business—the constant anxiety connected with the management of so great a concern, and I may even say so vast an Emporium, as the Repository—not to mention me being up awfully late of a night, and perhaps partaking of a little more sherry wine than what is good for me—these circumstances, Sir, have been wearing away of the Old Man to the shadow of his former self.

You having kindly allowed me for to draw some of my wages in advance, I was free to choose my place of rest, and *Bradshaw* was my guide. (See Milton's " Parodies Lost.")

To the everlasting honour of human nature, the Prophet had received several pressing invitations for the autumn; as for instance, if the printers will kindly put it into a tabular form, like a correct card, so for to speak :—

NATURE OF INVITATION.	INVITATOR.	OBJECT.	OBJECTION.
Scotch.	His Grace.	Grouse.	Legs.
Welsh.	Sir Watkin.	Mountains.	Wind.
French.	L'Emperoor.	L'Exposishon.	Been.
Norfolkshire.	H R.H.	Partridge-birds.	Stale.

There was likewise my old impostor of a Relative, which after having lured me into Retail Trade, had still the cool impudence for to declare as he would "give me another chance, if I would come down and have a quiet week at his suburban willa." Him and his willa be blowed ! *I* know what *that* means ; it means early hours, it means him locking up the cellarette, it means NICHOLAS never having that final tumbler, or so, which is essential to an Old Man's health at the Prophet's period.

All things considered, the Aged One thought as he could not do better than move, by easy stages, from one fashionable maritime resort to another, taking care, wherever he went, for to uphold the honour of the New Serious as your Confidential Representative and Sportive Editor.

Everywhere, when I arrived, I found that the periodical was respected; and which it stands to reason as it must have been respected still more so on my departure. Between ourselves, I think as it is very likely a completely new system of Hotel Reform may have been inaugurated by your Sportive Editor; for instead of paying their bills on the spot and without a murmur, which would only encourage extortion, I told every landlord as he had better send his bill to the Office, Number Eighty, Fleet Street, London, E.C., where *you*, my dear young Friend, will have an opportunity of seeing them, of comparing them, and of bringing the matter before the public mind in such case as you should consider any of them exorbitant.

One charge, however, certainly requires a little explanation, or else might seem excessive. You will find, in the Brighton accounts, *one* where it says, "Bed, 5s.; Attendance, 2s.; Brandy-and-water, 78s."—in all, Sir, amounting to £4 5s. 0d. Do not imagine, my dear young Friend, as those seventy-eight tumblers were *all* consumed by NICHOLAS. There were six of us as had all been over to the Races; and when you divide by six, especially considering the heat of the weather,

I am still in hopes as you will not think I had too much.

The best of sea-air is that you can take almost any quantity of refreshment without its hurting you.

I will write you again, if I am in want of money; but what with the system of Hotel Reform which I have adopted, and what with the general public's eagerness to stand treat to the celebrated Mr. NICHOLAS, which I have had the name put conspicuous on my little travelling trunk, my expenses hitherto in ready cash have been far more moderate than what you would expect.

It is time for to go and sit down in a chair on the Parade, for to get an appetite.   NICHOLAS.

NICHOLAS ON CROAKY.

Of what is the Old Man thinking?—Popular Ballad.

OUT FOR MY HOLIDAYS.

MY DEAR YOUNG FRIEND,—The Old Man was thinking, Sir, as it was high time for me to send a contry-bution to the first number of the Sixth Volume of your New Serious, when he was delighted for to perceive by a friendly missive, which it reached me through a private channel, as you were yourself quite of the same opinion. In fact, my dear young Friend, you put it even more forcible than what I could have done so myself, where you capitally say as my conduct is disgraceful. This, Sir, is the true frankness of the Anglo-Saxonian gentleman, than whom I am sure as I have always considered you one of them, though a little too apt for to blow up men as are more than twice your age. I fancied, Sir, as I could hear the very tones of your familiar voice in that sweet passage where the letter says as I am " a delusive old vagabond, on whom no reliance can be placed." You are not the only person which may have said so ; but what I am sincerely grateful for is the friendly way in which the communication is made, where you say that if I do not send you some copy you will have me locked up for obtaining of money under false pretences. Nothing, Sir, could be more frank, nor straightforwarder, nor more calculated for to put NICHOLAS on his mettle.

To say as I have been doing much execution among the partridge-birds, Sir, would be entirely useless, as I am sure you would not believe me, and therefore abstain from telling you a systematic falsehood ;—but I *have* been winning laurels, so for to speak, in another sphere, and which it is more adapted for the Prophet's present period of life, not to speak of my future.

I allude, Sir, to the delightful game of Croaky—or, as the French say, Croquet ; but I always pronounce it personally in the way which I have spelled it first.

Had I the pen, Sir, of a Captain Mayne Routledge, or a Mr. Edmund Reid, or of a gentleman to whom Shakespeare alludes as " the melancholy Jaques," which it strikes the Old Man as being rather like taking a liberty for to call him so, I would then, Sir, expatiate on the rules of the game, though what after all is the use of doing so when no two people can be found who play exactly alike ; but this is a digression. Full stop.

The Old Man, however, never sparing trouble nor expense when he sees a chance of affording combined amusement and instruction to the readers of your valuable New Serious, will give you a sketch of

1. Get the Marchioness to bring out a chair for you, so as you may not have to walk about the ground more than what is convenient.

2. Get her for to mix you a glass of cold brandy-and-water. *Note.*—There are some grounds where this is considered low. What's the odds?

3. Say you won't play until the next game, as **you** like to see the young people enjoying themselves.

4. See the young people enjoying themselves, **and** drink the cold brandy-and-water.

5. Send for another glass. *Note.*—Some players go to sleep at this stage of the game, but it is not obligatory for to do so. Suit yourself.

6. Take a weed, and wait till the game is over.

7. Take a mallet, and wait till the game begins.

8. Be particularly careful not to hit your ball through the first hoop.

9. Same as No. 8. *Note.*—The advantage of this plan, which is seldom recommended by less experienced authors, is that you can stay close to your chair where the cold brandy-and-water is.

10. Stay close to your chair where the cold brandy-and-water is.

11. A good strong pair of spectacles will help you in watching the darlings when they put their dear little boots——but NICHOLAS, NICHOLAS, you have a reputation for morality, my boy! Sustain it.

12. Say you are afraid the grass is getting damp, beg to be excused, go indoors, and have some more brandy-and-water.

REMARKS.

It will be seen as this Manwal is free from tedious

technicalities, and likewise from wrangling discussions about the mere minutiæ of the game. It is enough for the young player to learn the general principles of Croaky.

If these brief but well-considered remarks should help to inspire any one with a real affection for the noble game—and if, above all, they should tend to wipe away a tear from the cheeks of Innocence, whilst alleviating the hardships of the poor, they will have more than fulfilled the fondest aspirations of

NICHOLAS HIMSELF.

A VOICE FROM NICHOLAS AT SEA.

A bottle has been forwarded to our office. The bottle is not precisely empty, inasmuch as it contains what purports to be a communication from our eccentric contributor, NICHOLAS. In every other respect, however, it is as empty as a bottle could possibly be. The label on it bears the legend "Sherry Wine." We hasten to lay this remarkable document before our readers.

THE ATLANTIC OCEAN, IN THE MIDST OF THE EQUALNOXIOUS GALES.

MY DEAR YOUNG FRIEND,—If, by any possibility, this bottle should meet the eye of Mr. Frank Buckland, than whom a more vivacious man of science, nor yet a more truly rural ostreacultural ostreaculturalist, though a little gay—and when I say "meet his eye," NICHOLAS do not suppose as he will be out bathing and diving, and that this peculiar medium of postal communication will bob right up against his optic just as he emerges for to have a sort of a blow—and when I say "a sort of a blow," the Old Man does not mean as the bottle should hit him, but more after the manner of a whale,—Mr. B. will, perhaps, be so good enough for to send it to the Office of Fun, and which he knows where it is.

The Prophet, Sir, had been wallowing in the lapses of luxury to such an extent that he had pretty well nigh forgotten the necessity of predicting the winner of the St. Leger. This morning, for instance, there was me and Reginald de Courcy and little Spiffins set out from Ventnor for a day's sea-fishing. Spiffins—which his father made his money in retail trade, and accordingly Spiff. calls every man a " cad " which is hard-up, as I may have been myself, Sir—was only too proud, nevertheless, for to come out along of a territorial swell like Reginald, and a literary celebrity like me ; and so, for to amuse him, we let him pay the expenses, and likewise bring worms for bait.

Log.

10.30 *a.m.* — Wind, Sou'ard-by-West-Westerly. Chorus, Far, far upon the sea. Sentiment, The Memory of the late Lord Nelson. Toast, Here's the Wind that blows, and the Ship that goes, and the Lass that loves a sailor ! Pushed off. Set sail.

10.35.—Made an observation. Reading of it taken by Reginald, as follows :—" Spiff., hand over a corkscrew, and look after the worms, will you ?"

11.3.—The stormy winds did blow, did blow, and the stormy winds *do* blow ! Spiff. engaged in fixing the bait on the lines. Reginald and me was a-smoking, so for to speak.

11.10.—Opened a bottle of sherry wine. Told Spiff. as he *might* have some, if so be as he insisted upon it, but which he had much better attend to the worms.

Memorandum.—Spiff. ain't much of a good sailor, when all's said and done.

11.30.—Began for to fish. Me and Reginald took it easy, so for to speak, and let little Spiff. attend to the lines. What beautiful lines, for instance, were those made by Dr. Watts: " How does the busy little Spiff. Improve each shining minute ! He goes a-fishing in a skiff, Ri fol de rol de rol ! " Spiff. ain't much of a good sailor, though.

11.35.—Say what they will, the rolling motion of a small sailing-boat is much more adapted for a stupid young fool like Spiff., or for a robust member of the territorirorial aristocracy like Reginald, than what it is for a man of literary genius, meaning me. They were very good to me, both of 'em ; and which I am afraid as it was partly my own fault, the Prophet having imprudently said as he was fond of a short chopping sea, like what there is around me at the present moment —oh Lord, oh Lord !

11.40.—They say it does you good though.

11.45.—It *may* be doing me good. I dare say as it is. I will humbly endeavour for to believe so. But I wish as it would *not* do me good in this here particular way.

12.0.—*Noon, at Meridium.*—There are worse fellows in the world than little Spiff., likewise than Reginald. They have put things over me ; and they have likewise put things into me, so for to speak. Cognac. Sherry wine. Bottled Beer. Sherry wine. Bottled Beer. Cognac. Old Man 'll have a sleep.

Post Meridium.

If, by any possibility, this bottle should meet the

eye of Mr. Frank Buckland—and which perhaps I may as well clean it out first of all, by partaking of the sherry wine which it contains—let him tell the Editor as I was constant to my duties up to the very last. I am miserably, hopelessly, and desperately ill. I do not think as I shall ever live for to get ashore. I am certain that, if I should, no earthly power will **ever** again induce me for to venture on the watery deep. But, if even this Prophecy should prove my last, I *will* tell my dear young Friend and the general public, of whom I don't think much, that the following is the

CORRECT TIP FOR THE LEGER.

Achievement 1
The Hermit 2
Julius 3

I solemnly commit this bottle to the deep. Time will show whether the Vision which came to me whilst Slumbering on the Ocean was, or was not, Fallacious.

NICHOLAS.*

· * Curiously enough, this was to be Nicholas's last contribution, though it was not intended to be at the time it was written.—T. H.

MISCELLANEOUS PIECES.

BRINGING UP THE GUNS.

" THE battle, they say, will be lost or won,
  Ere our guns can be brought to the brow of the hill;
But, at least, we can try, so, forward all,
  And work, my men, cheerily—work with a will."

It was thus, on a beautiful morn in May,
  That our ruddy-faced, white-haired colonel spoke.
The valley below us was bright with spring.
  The hills above us were dim with smoke.

Then muscle and sinew we strained to the full,
  We were panting and grimy and grim with sweat;
But ever our colonel cheered us on,
  With " Courage, my lads, we shall reach them yet !"

All silently striving, we laboured along,
  The noise of the battle was loud on our ears.
One, *one* more effort—the guns are up,
  And the soldiers greet us with frantic cheers.

Ay, well they might ! They were sorely pressed,
  But our guns have speedily something to say;
And we watched our colonel quietly smile,
  As he saw that his regiment saved the day.

Through the hostile columns we sent our shot,
  We marked them waver, and break, and fly.
Just then, our gallant old colonel fell,
  And oh, 'twas a beautiful death to die !

LEARNING THE VERBS.

"SIGNIFYING TO BE, TO DO, OR TO SUFFER."

"To be?" Well, I followed the track,
   That gave me a chance of existence;
But I honestly own, looking back,
   That it's prettiest viewed from a distance.
Just now it seems easy and bright,
   But I haven't forgotten my scrambles
Over horrible rocks, or the night
   That I spent in the midst of the brambles.
     At times from the path I might stray,
       And thus make the journeying rougher;
     But still I was learning the way,
       "To Be, or to Do, or to Suffer!"

"To do?" I have worked rather hard,
   And my present position is cosy;
But I haven't done much as a Bard,
   And my prose—well, of course it is prosy!
The schemes and the aims of my youth
   Have long from old Time had a floorer,
And I doubt—shall I tell you the truth?
   If the world be a penny the poorer!
     If you cannot your vanity curb,
       You must either, my friend, be a duffer,
     Or you haven't yet learnt that a verb
       Is "To Be, or to Do, or to Suffer!"

"To suffer?" I took my degrees
   Long ago in that branch of our knowledge,
Where our hearts and our hopes are the fees,
   And the universe serves as a college.
I have had, as it is, rather more
   Than the usual share of affliction;
And that much is remaining in store
   Is my very decided conviction.
     But I find myself growing with years,
       Insensibly tougher and tougher;
     I can manage, I think, without tears,
       "To Be, and to Do, and to Suffer!"

I have stated the facts of the case,
    But heaven forbid I should grumble;
And I need not complain of a place
    That suits my capacities humble.
I have learnt how " to be "—well, a man :
    How " to do "—well, a part of my duty :
And in " suffering," own that the Plan
    Of the World is all goodness and beauty !
        Still at times from the path I may stray,
           And thus make the journeying rougher;
        But, at least, I am learning the way
           " To Be, and to Do, and to Suffer ."

THE TONIC TREATMENT OF DISEASE.

" The tonics which Mr. Skey so strongly recommends are curative rather as food than as medicine. They supply a want in the bodily system, just as wine supplies it ; and, in fact, wine is the chief of the tonics which Mr. Skey recommends. ' I consider wine, he says, ' indispensible to the tonic treatment of disease.' "—*Times*, 5th February, 1867.

WHATEVER your complaint may be,
    Neuralgic or pulmonic,
" The golden rule," says Doctor Skey,
    " Is still that wine's a tonic,
Men were by Nature's kindly plan
    To drink as well as *eat* meant ;"
A valetudinarian,
    I like this Tonic Treatment !

To persons in a mild decline,
    No matter how they *got* ill,
The Doctor recommends the wine,
    And not the physic-bottle.
To cure all natural ills was grog—
    The hot and strong and sweet—meant ;
And *that*, combined with wholesome prog,
    Is just the Tonic Treatment.

Says Skey, " My pupil, Mr. Jones,
   Ne'er fails in amputations ;
Ere cutting through a patient's bones,
   He plies him with libations !"
Suppose my arms want cutting short,
   Or else I find my feet meant,
Friend Jones prescribes a pint of port,
   And *that's* the Tonic Treatment !

In Jersey now does Jones reside,
   And, if I *were* a cripple,
I should, I think, feel gratified
   To know I'd had my tipple.
This little secret of the craft
   Is but for the discreet meant,
Though doubtless Mr. Jones is chaffed
   About the Tonic Treatment.

Our convalescence soon will be
   A period rather merry ;
" Throw physic to the dogs !" says Skey,
   " And stick to port and sherry !
But let's remember we were not
   To take our brandy *neat* meant ;
The person need not be a sot
   Who tries the Tonic Treatment."

By sober use of good old wine,
   The invalid's a gainer :
Two fools they are—the drunken swine,
   And the precise abstainer.
Man never was to reel about,
   Or stagger in the street, meant ;
Though there are perils which, no doubt,
   Attend the Tonic Treatment !

JUST a simple little story I've a fancy for inditing;
    It shows the funny quarters in which chivalry may
        lodge;
A story about Africa, and Englishmen, and fighting,
    And an unromantic hero by the name of Samuel
        Hodge.

"Samuel Hodge!" The words in question never pre-
        viously filled a
    Conspicuous place in Fiction or the chronicles of Fame;
And the Blood and Culture critics, or the Rosa and
        Matilda
    School of Novelists would shudder at the mention of
        the name!

It was up the Gambia River—and of *that* unpleasant
        station
    It is chiefly in connection with the fever that we
        hear!—
That my hero with the vulgar and prosaic appellation,
    Was a private—mind, a private—and a sturdy pioneer.

It's a dreary kind of region, where the river-mists
        arising
    Roll slowly out to seaward, dropping poison in their
        track;
And accordingly few gentlemen will find the fact sur-
        prising
    That a rather small proportion of our garrison comes
        back!

It is filthy, it is fetid, it is sordid, it is squalid;
    If you tried it for a season, you would very soon repent;
But the British trader likes it, and he finds a reason solid
    For the liking, in his profit at the rate of cent. per cent.

And, to guard the British trader, gallant men and merry
        younkers,
    In their coats of blue or scarlet, still are stationed at
        the post,

Whilst the migratory natives who are known as " Tillie-
    bunkas,"
  Grub up and down for ground-nuts, and chaffer on
    the coast.

Furthermore, to help the trader in his laudable vocation,
  We have heaps of little treaties with a host of little
    kings,
And, at times, the coloured caitiffs, in their wild in-
    ebriation,
  Gather round us, little hornets, with uncomfortable
    stings.

Then of course we have to *smoke* them ; and we do it
    with such vigour
  That the sooty rascals tremble, and a new allegiance
    swear ;
And—it's horrible to think of!—but we often shoot a
    nigger,
  Like that execrable tyrant, the atrocious Mr. Eyre !

To my tale :—The King of Barra had been getting rather
    " sarsy"—
  In fact, for such an insect, he was coming it too
    strong :
So we sent a small detachment—it was led by Colonel
    D'Arcy—
  To drive him from his capital at Túbabécolong !

Now on due investigation, when his land they had
    invaded,
  They learnt from information which was brought them
    by the guides
That the worthy King of Barra had completely *Barra-
    caded*
  The spacious mud-construction where his Majesty
    resides.

" At it, boys !" said Colonel D'Arcy, and himself was
    first to enter,
  And his fellows tried to follow with the customary
    cheers ;

Through the town he dashed impatient, but had scarcely
    reached the centre
  Ere he found the task before him was a task for
    Pioneers.

For so strongly and so stoutly all the gates were
    palisaded,
  The supports could never enter if he did not clear a
    way :—
But our Samuel Hodge, perceiving how the foe might
    be "persuaded,"
  Had certain special talents, which he hastened to
    display.

Whilst the bullets, then, were flying and the bayonets
    were glancing,
  Whilst the whole affair in fury rather heightened than
    relaxed,
Then with axe in hand, and silently, our Pioneer,
    advancing,
  SMOTE THE GATE; AND BADE IT OPEN; AND IT DID; AS
    IT WAS AXED!

L'ENVOI.

Just a word of explanation—it may save us from a
    quarrel;
  I have really no intention—'twould be shameful if I
    had!
Of preaching you a blatant, democratic kind of moral,
  For the "swell, you know," the D'Arcy, fought as
    bravely as the "cad!"

Yet I own that sometimes thinking how a courtier's
    decoration
  May be won by shabby service or disreputable dodge,
I regard with more than pleasure—with a sense of
    consolation—
  The Victoria Cross "For Valour" on the breast of
    Samuel Hodge!

THE PACE THAT KILLS.

THE gallop of life was once exciting,
   Madly we dashed over pleasant plains;
And the joy like the joy of a brave man fighting
   Poured in a flood through our eager veins
Hot youth is the time for the splendid ardour
   That stings and startles, that throbs and thrills;
And ever we pressed our horses harder,
   Galloping on at the pace that kills!

So rapid the pace, so keen the pleasure,
   Scarcely we paused to glance aside,
As we mocked the dullards who watched at leisure
   The frantic race that we chose to ride.
Yes, youth is the time when a master passion,
   Or Love or Ambition, our nature fills;
And each of us rode in a different fashion—
   All of us rode at the pace that kills!

And vainly, oh, friends, ye strive to bind us;
   Flippantly, gaily, we answer *you*:
" Should Atra Cura jump up behind us,
   Strong are our steeds, and can carry two!"
But we find the road so smooth at morning,
   Rugged at night 'mid the lonely hills;
And all too late we recall the warning,
   Weary too late of the pace that kills!

       *   *   *   *

The gallop of life was just beginning;
   Strength we wasted in efforts vain;
And now, when the prizes are worth the winning,
   We've scarcely the spirit to ride again!
The spirit, forsooth! 'Tis our *strength* has failed us,
   And sadly we ask, as we count our ills,
" What pitiful, pestilent folly ailed us?
   Why did we ride at the pace that kills?"

THE CITY OF PRAGUE.

Scene: " Bohemia: a desert country near the sea."—SHAKESPEARE.

I DWELT in a city enchanted,
    And lonely, indeed, was my lot;
Two guineas a week, all I wanted,
    Was certainly all that I got.
Well, somehow I found it was plenty;
    Perhaps you may find it the same,
If—*if* you are just five-and-twenty,
    With industry, hope, and an aim:
        Though the latitude's rather uncertain,
          And the longitude also is vague,
      The persons I pity who know not the city,
        The beautiful City of Prague!

Bohemian of course were my neighbours,
    And not of a pastoral kind!
Our pipes were of clay, and our tabors
    Would scarcely be easy to find.
Our Tabors?   Instead of such mountains,
    Ben Holborn was all we could share,
And the nearest available fountains
    Were the horrible things in the square:
        Does the latitude still seem uncertain?
          Or think ye the longitude vague?
      The persons I pity who know not the city,
        The beautiful City of Prague!

How we laughed as we laboured together!
    How well I remember, to-day,
Our " outings" in midsummer weather,
    Our winter delights at the play!
We were not over-nice in our dinners;
    Our " rooms" were up rickety stairs;
But if hope be the wealth of beginners,
    By Jove we were all millionaires!
        Our incomes were very uncertain,
          Our prospects were equally vague;
      Yet the persons I pity who know not the city,
        The beautiful city of Prague!

If at times the horizon was frowning,
   Or the ocean of life looking grim,
Who dreamed, do you fancy, of drowning?
   Not we, for we knew we could swim . . .
Oh, Friends, by whose side I was breasting
   The billows that rolled to the shore,
Ye are quietly, quietly resting,
   To laugh and to labour no more!
     Still, in accents a little uncertain,
      And tones that are possibly vague,
     The persons I pity who know not the city,
     The beautiful City of Prague!

L'ENVOI.

As for me, I have come to an anchor;
   I have taken my watch out of pawn;
I keep an account with a banker,
   Which at present is *not* overdrawn.
Though my clothes may be none of the smartest,
   The " snip " has receipted the bill;
But the days I was poor and an artist
   Are the dearest of days to me still!
     Though the latitude's rather uncertain,
      And the longitude also is vague,
     The persons I pity who know not the city,
     The beautiful City of Prague!

My Lost Old Age.

BY A YOUNG INVALID.

I'm only nine-and-twenty yet,
    Though young experience makes me sage;
So how on earth can *I* forget
    The memory of my lost old age?
Of manhood's prime let others boast;
    It comes too late, or goes too soon;
At times, the life I envy most
    Is that of slippered pantaloon!

In days of old—a twelvemonth back!—
    I laughed, and quaffed, and chaffed my fill;
And now, a broken-winded hack,
    I'm weak and worn, and faint and ill.
Life's opening chapter pleased me well;
    Too hurriedly I turned the page;
I spoiled the volume . . . . Who can tell
    What *might* have been my lost old age?

I lived my life; I had my day;
    And now I feel it more and more,
The game I have no strength to play
    Seems better than it seemed of yore.
I watch the sport with earnest eyes,
    That gleam with joy before it ends;
For plainly I can hear the cries
    That hail the triumph of my friends.

We work so hard, we age so soon,
    We live so swiftly, one and all,
That ere our day be fairly noon
    The shadows eastward seem to fall.
Some tender light may gild them yet;
    As yet, it's not so *very* cold;
And, on the whole, I *won't* regret
    My slender chance of growing old!

THE DROUGHT AND THE RAIN.

I.—DROUGHT.

THE lips of Earth the Mother was black;
They gaped through fissure and crevice and crack;
  O for the fall of the rain!
And the life of the flowers paused; and the wheat,
That was rushing up seemed to droop in the heat,
And its grass-green blades, they yearned for the sweet,
  The sweet, sweet kiss of the rain!

The secular cypress, solemn and still,
The sentinel pine on the edge of the hill,
  Watched, but they watched in vain;
And the glare on the land, the glare on the sea,
The glare on terrace, and tower, and tree,
Grew fiercer and fiercer, mercilessly:
  O for the fall of the rain!

The streams were silent, the wells were dry,
The pitiless clouds passed slowly by,
  With never a drop of rain.
The priests in the town exhumed a saint,
They passed in procession with prayers and paint,
But the heavens were cruel, or faith was faint:
  Came never a drop of rain.
  O for the fall of the rain!

II.—THE RAIN.

One night the lift grew ragged and wild.
With a sound like the lisp and the laugh of a child
 Fell the first sweet drops of the rain!
Moist lips of the mist the mountain kissed,
 And cooled the hot breath of the plain;
The emerald wheat leapt gaily to meet
 The welcome kiss of the rain;
And the roses around, as they woke at the sound,
 Broke into blossom again:
 O beautiful, bountiful rain!

SOUNDING THE RECALL.

"On bat le rappel là-haut!"—ALFRED MURGER.

SINCE men are not fashioned like cattle,
  They struggle and suffer and sin ;
They push to the front of the battle,
  Determined to conquer or win.
Do I seek to diminish that ardour ?
  I answer you, mournfully, No :
But the battle gets harder and harder—
    Listen ! *On bat,*
  On bat le rappel là-haut !

Our little Bohemian legion
  Expected no conqueror's arch,
And we trudged through a desolate region,
  And often were faint on the march.
Round the bivouac fire we assembled,
  That fire was uncertain and low ;
As our eyelids were closing, we trembled ;
    Listen ! *On bat,*
  On bat le rappel là-haut !

There was one of our band whom we cherished—
  The youngest, the purest, the best ;—
In the frost of the night-time he perished,
  Going quietly home to his rest ;*
And we thought, as we buried our dear one,
  And mournfully turned us to go,
That the summons was still sounding near one—
    Listen ! *On bat,*
  On bat le rappel là-haut !

O the joys of the past !   The caresses,
  The kisses from lips that are cold,
The eyes that were blue, and the tresses
  That waved with a ripple of gold !
We have lived, we have loved, we have spoken
  Hot words that set hearts in a glow ;
And now we are weary and broken,—
    Listen ! *On bat,*
  On bat le rappel là-haut !

      * Paul Gray, obiit Nov. 14, 1866.

TURN OF THE TIDE.

THE tides of life had ebbed so low,
I deemed they might forget to flow;
Weary alike of hope and fear
    I lay, methought, a-dying.
Some love of living moved me yet;
One feeble sigh, one faint regret,
Breathing, I paused :—and seemed to hear
    Another breath replying.

It freshened, freshened—clear and keen,
It reached me, and a peace serene
Fell on dull heart and weary frame
    And cooled my pulses burning :—
The sun shone out on wavelets blue;
The sea's familiar voice I knew ;—
Over the sands of death they came,
    The tides of life returning.

And marvellous it seems once more
To rest upon life's sunny shore,
Cheerily listening to the song
    The merry waves are making :—
Thankful, I slumber, sure indeed
That, should the tide again recede,
Heavenly voices will, ere long,
    Salute a happier waking.

P. P. C.

MY shattered strength is failing quite,
    But, as it ebbs away,
I pass toward the tranquil night
    That brings the brighter day.

The pain is somewhat hard to bear,
    But harder yet must be,
Ere any dreams or doubts shall tear
    My heart, O God, from Thee.

With pain I draw my faintest breath—
  A poor and paltry strife ;
I own, I feel my Life is Death,
  But Death shall give me Life.

A hundred darling memories float
  Across my mind at night ;
I count them vainly o'er by rote
  When pain comes back with light.

And bitter, bitter grows the thought
  When 'neath the rising sun,
I mind the sins that I have wrought,
  The evil I have done.

" Our Father " spares the very worst,
  There yet is hope for me ;
I know I said " Our Father " first
  Beside my mother's knee.

[NOTE :—The last three poems are here published for the first time.]

THE END.

F. BENTLEY AND CO., PRINTERS, LONDON.

www.ingramcontent.com/pod-product-compliance
Lightning Source LLC
Chambersburg PA
CBHW020234030726
47497CB00009B/3085